A CRAZY SECOND CHANCE

JULIA EVANS

CONTENTS

SERIOUSLY…NO…IT CAN'T BE

He always treated me like a dirty little secret.
And now he's my boss.

Twelve years ago, John McQueen promised we'd stay friends after
one delicious night together.
It's impossible to forget his god-like body and piercing blue eyes.

But after being bullied so much, I couldn't.
Getting your heart broken time after time never feels good.

What's that saying?
It hurts me to hate him,
But loving him is worse.

And now I have to work for him.
I wonder if he's still the same tempting, awful jerk I fell for.

At this point in my life,
With eviction and debt burying me alive,
I don't have an option but to put my big girl panties on,

And accept the job.

I thought not falling in love with him again was going to be my only
obstacle
Boy was I wrong.
Seems like he has a little secret of his own...

1

LUCY

I stare at the piece of paper in my hand in disbelief, hot tears pricking behind my eyes. I feel light-headed and dizzy, and realize I've stopped *breathing*. I feel like I'm going to throw up or pass out. I have to get out of here, now.

As I run through the lobby of the office, heading straight for the huge double glass doors — the same doors I was so thrilled and so proud to first walk through just three short months ago — I vaguely hear a voice calling out after me.

"Lucy, wait!" my supervisor Brett shouts, his tone frazzled. "That's not how you were supposed to find out, I sent you an email for a meeting —"

But I barely hear him as the sound of blood rushing to my head drowns out his voice. I burst through the doors and into the street, breaking into a run without a second thought. You would think people would stop and stare at a girl darting down the sidewalk in a skirt and heels with makeup and tears running down her face, but this is Chicago. No one glances twice as my nasty surge of adrenaline carries me past several blocks of dirty, crowded sidewalks. I'm hardly the strangest thing they've seen in this city, even just today.

Finally, the combination of running and sobbing catches up to me, and I have to stop. I find myself standing on a random street corner, doubled over and gasping for air. I bend over with my head between my knees, trying to take deep breaths and calm myself down. I glance at my hand and realize I still have the paper, the one that just turned my entire life upside-down, clutched in my hand.

Sniffling, I smooth the paper against my skirt. Now the paper is crumpled and tear stained. I read through it again, desperately hoping I misread it, that there's some hope or light at the end of the tunnel. But as I peer through the saltwater of more unfallen tears in my eyes, I can see that the words haven't magically changed.

Dear Lucy Myers,

Due to circumstances beyond our control, we regret to inform you that your position at McGregor Publishing LLC has been made redundant. This decision has been made as a result of...

And just like moments ago in the office, I can't bring myself to finish the letter.

I can't believe this is happening to me.

I'm losing my job. Not *fired*, I can see as I skim further down the letter. *Laid off.* Laid off from my first real "big girl" job in the city, the job I was so, *so* proud of.

I remember going in for my first interview. I'd taken the train into the city from my parent's house in the suburbs and gotten a hotel. I was so nervous I thought I was going to have a panic attack. The second I walked through the front doors into the gleaming lobby, which was decorated with whimsical artwork from painted book pages, I knew this was the perfect place for me. I wanted this job so bad.

The moment I stepped into Brett's office and shook his hand, I felt more at ease. Brett is — or I guess, *was* — my immediate supervisor.

He works directly under Georgina, the head boss, leading a team of other junior editors. He's only a couple of years older than I am, tall and reedy, with unruly brown hair and glasses. And not those thick-framed, hipster glasses, either... the guy wears wire-framed spectacles with so much magnification his warm brown eyes look enormous, giving him the appearance of a Labrador. In fact, everything about Brett is floppy and sweet, just like a giant puppy.

He's kind, too. I know he would hate firing anyone on our team, and I believe what he said about not wanting me to find out that way. I missed work yesterday, a Monday, because I wasn't feeling well (an extremely rare occurrence, but I couldn't help it). I hadn't checked my email all weekend either. Brett probably emailed over the weekend, and I just didn't see it. When I came into work today, I headed straight for my office mailbox in the lobby, like I always do. I flipped through the usual stack of ads and notices before finding the foreboding envelope with my name on it.

I adore everything about my job. I love the gorgeous building, all the other junior editors, Brett, my cubicle with a window view, the sound the printer makes when it spits out a fresh manuscript. I've always wanted to work in publishing, so landing this as my first real job was simply a dream come true.

Now, I'm completely devastated. I'm losing more than just my job. This might cost me everything I've worked so hard for. Without a paycheck, how am I supposed to afford living in the city?

My best friend Jen and I moved to Chicago right after college. Jen was working as an intern for a fashion magazine the summer after graduation, taking the train into the city every day. The company offered her a full-time, paid position at the end of the summer, and she couldn't wait to get an apartment close to work due to the long commute. We always planned on living together and getting our dream jobs in the big city. So when she heard about another apartment in her building was available, all that was left to do was for me to land the right job.

I had enough money saved up from old jobs to cover the deposit and a month or two of expenses. But I was ready to use my degree and work for a publishing company. With visions of a 9-5, health insurance, and happy hours with fellow book-loving colleagues, I spent a month applying for jobs without luck. For the 20 jobs I applied for, I only got a couple interviews, and McGregor Publishing LLC was the first place that extended a job offer.

Without this job, I have nothing. No career, no money, no apartment, no big city, no Jen as a neighbor. I don't know what to do. So I do what I have always done in a crisis since junior year of high school. I call Jen.

"What's wrong?" Jen asks, picking up on the first ring. She already sounds worried. She knows I'm supposed to be working right now.

I can't even answer, I just burst into tears. Again. I'm a mess today.

"Oh, my God, Lucy, what is it? Are you okay? That was stupid. Sorry. You're obviously not okay, but like, are you safe? Where are you?"

"I... lost... my..." I sob quietly into my phone.

"You what? You lost something? What is it, Lucy? Whatever it is, we'll find it," Jen says soothingly.

"No, no, no!" I wail. "I... lost... my..."

"What, Lucy? What is it?"

"I lost my jooooob!" I lose it again at the admission, blubbering uncontrollably on the sidewalk. I'm sure I make for good entertainment on the streets of Chicago.

"Oh, no, Lucy, that sucks!" Jen's tone remains calm and maternal. I shudder with relief. I don't know why I was expecting anything else, because Jen is always kind and considerate. Toward me, at least.

"What am I going to do?" I say pitifully, feeling lost.

"You mean, what are *we* going to do? You're not in this alone, Lucy, I'll help you, of course. Now take some deep breaths. Are you at the office right now?"

I take my friend's advice, drawing a couple of slow, deep breaths and feeling myself start to calm down.

"No, I ran out," I confess, embarrassed.

"Okay, so first let's figure out what you are going to do right now. Do you think you can go back to work today?"

"No way." I think of Brett's face, feeling mortified. Outside of taking yesterday off, I rarely miss work, but there's no way I can pull myself together enough to go back to the office right now. Besides, what's the point? Who am I trying to impress? I've already lost my job.

"Okay, all right, that's fine," Jen says, and I can practically hear the wheels in her head spinning. That's one of the great things about Jen. She's so cool, calm, and collected. She's exactly who you would want on your team in an emergency. It's part of what makes her such an amazing friend. "Why don't you go home, enjoy a bath, eat something, and take a nap. Oh, and email me your resume. I'll look over it when I get a break today, and then I'll come home after work to watch crappy TV. We can get takeout and you can apply for some jobs online. My treat. How does that sound?"

"That sounds amazing," I sigh. "You're the best."

"Everything's going to work out, I promise."

"But what about rent and stuff? What if I have to move out? God, what if I have to move back in with my folks? I'll feel like such a loser!" I feel my anxiety rising again.

"That's not going to happen, and you can't worry about all that stuff now," Jen tells me firmly. "Just get through today, and we will figure out the rest together."

"Promise?" I add quietly.

"Swear to God. You've got a little bit of savings, right? And so do I. I'm sure you'll get a new job soon, even if you have to go back to working at a coffee shop or something part-time. And worst-case scenario, I can lend you rent money for a bit, but I doubt it will even come to that. This isn't the end of the world, Luce. Everything's going to be fine."

"What did I ever do to deserve a friend like you?" I already feel a thousand times better.

"Just remember this next time I need something," Jen jokes. "Now, go home, and I'll see you later, okay?"

"Okay," I nod, even though she can't see me. "Thanks, Jen. Seriously."

"It's nothing. See you tonight."

I shove my phone in my pocket, drawing another deep breath. I glance around the busy street and get my bearings. I'm not far from my apartment, so I break into a brisk walk.

Once I make it home, I toss my jacket and purse on the couch and head straight to the kitchen. I pour myself a generous glass of wine, even though it's still morning. I take a gulp and top the glass off before carrying it into the bathroom and placing it on the edge of the tub. I fill the tub with scalding hot water, pouring my expensive, special occasion oil in. After I scrub my face clean of makeup and tears at the sink, I lower my body into the comforting bubbles.

As the wine warms my insides and the water warms my skin, I tell myself that Jen is right, that everything is going to work out.

It has to.

I don't have any other option.

2

JOHN

"Perfect. Mmmhmm. Great. Yes, please have that on my desk by Monday morning." I lean back and whirl around in my chair (ergonomic, padded, and ridiculously expensive — a gift from the staff at last year's holiday party) as I end yet another conference call. Sometimes it seems like all I do is lead conference calls and respond to emails.

But I can't complain.

I stretch my arms above my head and gaze out the floor-to-ceiling window that composes the back wall of my office. I enjoy my job, my office, my staff. I appreciate how my assistant, Greta, brings coffee to my desk every morning, prepared just the way I like it without even being asked. The view of the sprawling city of Chicago from my skyscraper office is perfect. I love having an identity that isn't tied up in sports, but in something that actually requires my brain and my degree. I love owning something real, something I can be proud of, and make my family proud, too.

I might be the only guy in the world who used a full football scholarship to pay for a bachelor's degree in English, I muse to myself, watching people rush around on the street below me. From here, they look like tiny little dots, ants, scurrying about the grid of dirty sidewalks. It's crazy to think how all these people have no idea that I am looking down on them, rushing about their busy lives.

I glance across my desk at a framed photo, one of only two in my office. It's a picture of my parents and me at my high school graduation. I'm in a cap and gown, gripping my diploma in one hand and a football in the other. My parents are beaming, smiles stretched from ear to ear, but me? I look glum.

Football may have paid my way through college, but it was never my true passion. Truthfully, I would've done anything to get out from under Dad's thumb, at least financially. Luckily, or perhaps due to my dad's version of "discipline," I was really, really good at football. I would never have admitted it to him or anyone else at the time, but I would rather work on a poem or short story for a creative writing class than sprint laps or tackle on the field. Football was cool. Being an English nerd, especially as a jock, was decidedly *not cool*.

But toward the end of high school, I started to realize (with some help) that what other people — my dad included — thought didn't really matter. Being popular, voted prom king, dating the hottest girl in school — I had it all. Stuff that other guys would kill for. And none of it mattered.

I just wish I realized it a little sooner.

I think back to those days sometimes, and while I had, by most standards, a pretty ideal high school experience, I would have changed some things. Sometimes, popularity comes at a price, and I wasn't exactly the nicest guy. I was young and dumb, and I went along with things I shouldn't have to avoid making waves and to keep my social standing.

I chuckle to myself, thinking how much I've changed.

I feel bad for how I treated people then, certain people in particular who still stand out in my mind, but I was young. I'm sure they've forgotten all about me, the stereotypical high school jerk, jock bully, even though I'll always remember them.

And it's not like I can complain about how my life turned out, at least so far. In college, I took what I learned about people and what matters in life and tried to be a better person. I still played football and took it seriously — it was, after all, how I funded my degree. As much resentment as I had, and maybe even still possess a bit, toward my old man for pushing me so hard, I'll always be grateful. Football allowed me to pay for the future I have now.

Not that my folks couldn't have afforded college if I hadn't gotten a scholarship. But I'm pretty sure my Dad would've disowned me if I hadn't received an athletic scholarship. It was a huge point of pride for him. I heard him bragging to his buddies about it all the time back then. "Yeah, you know, Johnny Boy got a full ride. Yep, from football. Yeah, I coached him pretty well, if I do say so myself." It was so like him, to take credit for *my* achievement.

Did I feel bad for potentially taking a scholarship away from someone who really needed it? Someone who loved football, or someone who wouldn't be able to afford it otherwise? Sure, all the time. I hated telling anyone I'd gotten a scholarship. It was clear from my clothes, car, and everything else that I didn't *need* it.

I decided no matter what career path I ended up taking, I would earn enough money to start my own scholarship at my alma mater. So that's exactly what I did a few years ago, shortly after I became owner and CEO of Room Publishing Company.

How does a star football player on an athletic scholarship become the head of a publishing company? Well, like I said, I made a conscious effort to become a better person, and that meant I had to be myself, even if it didn't make me "cool."

One of the best things about college, though, was that those labels didn't exist anymore. Or maybe they did, but they mattered a whole lot less once you were leaving your teen years behind and entering the adult world. Life quickly becomes about who you are, what job you see yourself doing, and what kind of life you want to lead, and less about what you're wearing, who you're dating, or which parties you're invited to.

Although I still played football out of financial obligation, I started to pursue my real interests in college. I'd always enjoyed English class; it came naturally to me.

Once in high school, a teacher selected my essay to read aloud to the class.

"I want you all to pay close attention," she said, pulling her spectacles up from a chain that held them around her neck and resting them on her long, thin nose. I can picture her perfectly, but I've long since forgotten her name. "One of your classmates wrote this, and it's truly a beautiful example of prose. *This* is the caliber of writing I'm looking for in all of your assignments." She clutched a paper in hand and I sank into my seat, bored and ready to hear another cheesy love poem by one of the girls. My cheeks flushed with pride and embarrassment when she started reading and I recognized my own words flowing out of her mouth. When she finished and told the class I wrote it, I got so much shit from the other guys. *Nerd,* they said. *Dork. Dweeb.*

Because in high school, you couldn't be multidimensional. Others want to put you in a category, in a box. Jock, nerd, theater kid, cheerleader, skater, art freak, druggie, loser. You couldn't be both a jock like my old buddy Boomer, and an English nerd like my former best friend Mikey. You couldn't fit into two categories. When you tried to dip your toe into another box, it made people uncomfortable; they didn't know how to categorize you anymore.

Jock always won out over nerd, every time. It was just easier to stay in my lane.

I stayed after class that day and approached the teacher, head down. I asked her to please not read my work out loud to the class anymore, or at least not say it was mine.

"Why on earth wouldn't you want to take credit for your work?" she asked, perplexed. "You should be proud of your writing, John. You are advanced beyond your years, and certainly beyond the level of most of your peers."

"It's hard to explain," I replied gruffly. "But can you please just not read my stuff anymore? Or like, at least not mention my name?"

She'd taken off her spectacles at that and looked me right in the eye. A long pause passed between us, as if she was measuring her words and deciding what to say next.

"Of course, John," she agreed finally. "I will honor your request. But you should really think about what matters in life, and what matters to you. You're an excellent writer, and I would hate to see all that natural talent and hard work go to waste."

"Thanks," I muttered, eager to break her intense eye contact. That teacher's name may escape me, but her words in that moment never will.

In college, I refused to be embarrassed by my passions or my talents. I didn't want to waste any more time on things or people I didn't like or care about. I loaded up on creative writing courses my first semester, taking every English class possible. I declared English as my major before classes even started, and although most other students I knew switched their major at least once, I never did.

I also received a minor in business. I knew I wanted to pursue some sort of career leveraging my English degree, but I also wanted to possess my own business. I was still popular in college, I guess, but it just wasn't my focus anymore. I got invited to parties, and I went to several. But if it came down to partying or studying for an English exam, I chose studying — something I never would have been willing to risk in high school.

I might be a nerd now, I thought, looking at the shelf full of books in my office, but *I'm certainly not a loser*. And as it turns out, being a nerd makes me pretty fucking happy.

And, well, *rich*. Richer than my parents, even.

So as much as Dad would prefer me to be a famous athlete, he can't help but be proud of me for being a wealthy CEO and business owner.

Not so bad for a nerd, huh?

My cell phone buzzes from where it's sitting on my desk, pulling me out of my reverie. I pick it up, glancing at the screen before answering. Olivia. I sigh to myself, knowing I have no choice but to answer.

"Hello?" I answer gruffly, hoping to make this call quick.

"Hi, Daddy!" chirps a little voice. My shoulders immediately relax, and a relieved smile passes across my face.

"Hi, Bella baby," I say. "How's it going? Hang on," I pull my phone away from my face to check the time. "Wait, how come you're not at school?"

"Mommy said no school today!" my four-year-old daughter sings sweetly into the phone. "She says we're playing hockey!"

"Hockey?" I furrow my brow, puzzled. "But you don't play... wait, you mean hooky?"

"Hooky! Hooky! Hooky!" Bella repeats, giggling. I roll my eyes up towards the ceiling. Why the hell isn't Bella at school? Don't get me wrong, I love hearing her voice, and I'm glad she called. But she is supposed to be at preschool.

"Where is your mother?"

"She's sleeping," Bella answers sweetly. "We were watching a movie and she started snoring, right on the couch! So I took her phone to play Candy Crush — oops!" Bella lowers her voice to a whisper. "Don't tell Mommy I played Candy Crush, Daddy, okay? It's not Screen Time yet," she says solemnly. I consider explaining that watching a movie involves a screen, too, but then think better of it.

"Okay, I won't, I promise," I whisper back conspiratorially.

"But then I got bored and I remembered I can call you on the phone! So I did! Because I miss you, Daddy!"

"I know, baby. I miss you too," I say sincerely. "But this is your week with your mom. You love your mom too, don't you?"

Bella doesn't say anything.

"Bella?"

"I'm nodding my head, Daddy," she says cheerfully, not understanding that I can't see her.

"And sometimes you miss Mommy when you stay with me, don't you?"

Silence again.

"Bella, are you nodding?"

"Yes, Daddy!"

"Okay. So have fun with Mommy, and you can always call and talk to me. But right now I need you to wake up Mommy and give her the phone, okay? I want to talk to her," I explain, even though talking to Olivia is the last thing I want to do.

"Okay, Daddy!" I hear muffled rustling as Bella sets the phone down. "Wake up, Mommy!" I hear her say in the background. I picture the living room at Olivia's house; our old house. She's probably fast asleep on the living room couch, curled up in a ball under some ungodly expensive cashmere throw blanket. I hear her grumbling as Bella hands her the phone. "Bella, go play in your room for a minute while I talk to your father, okay?" she whispers.

"Hi, John," she says silkily into the phone. "How nice of you to call."

"I didn't call, Olivia. Bella called me. Because you were asleep."

"Oh, come on, John, it was just a quick cat nap, and she is sitting right here with me. It's fine," says Olivia, growing defensive as usual.

"Okay, but why isn't Bella at school?"

"She didn't want to go," Olivia says simply.

"Oh, really?" I ask skeptically. Bella loves school. Preschool is all about playing, coloring, and singing songs. It's not exactly strenuous (for the kids, at least — God bless the teachers. I can't imagine wrangling a big group of toddlers all day), and Bella loves seeing all of her little friends every day. She has never once asked me to stay home from school.

"Well, she didn't say so, but I could tell," Olivia explains breezily. "Plus, you know..." she lowers her voice, and when she speaks again it comes out husky. The voice she used to use whenever she felt like having sex. "I've been... a little lonely, John. Maybe you could come by one night this week for dinner? I'll make your favorite... open a bottle of wine... put Bella to bed early... doesn't that sound nice?"

"No, it doesn't," I say bluntly. "If you're so bored and lonely, Olivia, why don't you, oh, I don't know, get a job, maybe?" This last part I say sarcastically, since it's a suggestion I've made a million times before.

"Now why would I do that? Don't you want me to be the very best mother I can for Bella? Isn't it better if I'm available for her?" Olivia asks indignantly.

I sigh. There's no winning with Olivia. I don't know why I bother trying to reason with her.

"Do you think you're being the very best mother by keeping her home from school just because you're bored?" I snap. I don't want to be harsh, but we're talking about my kid here.

"You don't know what it's like," says Olivia, her voice trembling. Oh boy, here come the waterworks. "It's hard being a single mother..." I listen to her cry and complain for a few minutes, resisting the temptation to point out that I'm a single father, and I hold a job, run a company, in fact, *and* manage to completely support her and our child.

Finally, I try to end the call on a good note.

"Okay, okay, I'm sorry for judging you. It's just important to me that Bella values her education. I know she's still little, but they learn early, you know?" I say gently.

"Well, isn't time with her mother important, too?" Olivia sniffs.

"Of course it is," I agree. "Just maybe not during school hours. Alright?"

"Whatever," Olivia sighs, neither agreeing nor disagreeing.

"Okay. Can I talk to Bella one more time?"

"Bella, come here, honey!" Olivia calls out, and I hear the pitter patter of Bella's feet running towards her. Before Olivia can say goodbye, Bella has grabbed the phone out of her hand.

"Hi, Daddy!"

"Hey, baby. I just wanted to make sure I said goodbye to you before hanging up with your mom."

"Okay. Bye bye, Daddy!"

"Bye bye, baby. Daddy loves you. So much," I say.

"Love you too, Daddy! Sooooooo much!" she giggles, then hangs up the phone.

3

LUCY

"Cheers!" I say giddily, reaching over to clink my very full glass against Jen's.

"To your new job!" says Jen excitedly before taking a swig. "I *knew* everything would work out!"

And she was right.

After being laid off, I spent a few days sulking around my apartment. I alternated between laying on the couch crying, drinking wine while binge-watching TV and binge-eating ice cream like I'd just been dumped, and drinking way too much coffee. So much that I thought I was going to have a panic attack while firing off dozens of online job applications.

I quickly started getting interview offers. Much more quickly, I noticed, than when I applied for jobs before moving into the city. I guess that even having just a few months of experience at a publishing company was my way in. With McGregor Publishing at the top of my resume, other publishing companies were giving me a chance.

I trudged up and down the streets of Chicago in what I had come to refer to as my "interview uniform," a simple black dress, a blazer, and black flats. I attempted heels, but after bandaging blisters on my toes and heels after the first day of marching around the city, I realized that flats would have to do. I've never been much of a heels kind of girl, anyway.

I can't even remember how many jobs I applied for in total. And not just with publishing companies, either. There are only so many of those, even in a big city like Chicago. I sent my resume to any company that had anything even remotely to do with books. I applied to countless libraries, bookstores, and even coffee shops that I knew had a few racks of books for sale. Being a barista may not have been what I envisioned as my career in the big city, but it would sure beat moving back in with my parents with my tail hanging between my legs. I doubt I could even afford to live on a barista's hourly wages, but it would be better than no income at all.

After hours of filling out applications and marching around town to interviews, I finally got a call back. It was from Room Publishing, my number one choice. Actually, I'd applied there before when I first moved to the city, the same time I applied for McGregor Publishing. The companies are very similar, but I like the books that come from Room Publishing a bit more. I filled out their online application, but never heard back from them at the time. I assume they weren't hiring then, but they must have an opening now.

And I got it!

"Hello, is this Lucy Myers?" said a woman's voice when I breathlessly answered the call from an unknown number. I just climbed out of the shower after finishing another day of interviews and applications and was standing in my room with dripping wet hair.

"Yes, this is Lucy," I answered, my voice trembling with hope.

"This is Greta with Room Publishing, we met at your interview?"

"Oh, yes. Hi, Greta," I responded nervously. I remember her, but only vaguely.

"We'd like to offer you the junior editor position here, starting Monday."

I did a little jig of excitement. "Thank you, that's wonderful news!" I said, trying to sound professional.

"I spoke with the owner of the company, John, and he agrees

you're perfect for the job. I apologize again that he wasn't there for your interview, but there was a scheduling conflict that couldn't be avoided."

I barely heard her words because I was so elated. Who cares about the owner? I hardly saw the head boss at my last job. Even if this guy is the worst person to work for, I would do whatever it takes to stay in my apartment and keep my dream job.

Greta continued to explain HR requirements, upcoming paper-work, and a formal email that I'd receive before the end of this week. I jotted down everything on a notepad by my bed, and as soon as she hung up, I screamed with glee. Dancing around my bedroom, I called Jen immediately.

"*Guess what*?!" I squealed into the phone, smiling so hard my cheeks hurt.

"You got another interview? Somewhere really good?" Jen asked hopefully.

"Better than that — I got a job!" I screech, flinging myself back-wards onto my bed and letting my towel fall around me.

"That's amazing!" Jen cheered. "That was so fast! I'm so proud of you! I told you everything would work out!"

"You were right!" I beamed.

"I'm leaving the office right now. We're going out to celebrate!"

It felt similar to the day three months ago when I received the job at McGregor. I dried my hair, brushing it until it gleamed, then threw on a short red dress and some makeup. I even painted my lips fire engine red to match my dress and kept my eye makeup simple to make my pouty mouth really pop.

When Jen came over later to get a cab with me, wearing a dress very similar to mine but in black, she looked me up and down and whistled.

"I'm glad you're in the mood to party," she said mischievously, wiggling her eyebrows at me. "Where do you want to go?"

"Oh, I don't care. Somewhere we can dance!"

"Got it."

We piled into the back of a cab, while Jen gave the driver directions to some club I've never been to before. After showing our ID to the burly bouncer at the door, we bee-lined straight to the bar and grabbed two barstools.

So now we are here, downing our first drinks of the night. I was so excited about the job earlier that I forgot to eat dinner, and the warm alcohol hits my empty stomach immediately, making me warm and tingly.

"So, you didn't even tell me yet, what's the new job?" asks Jen, swinging one long leg across the other, perched on her bar stool. "I know you filled out a billion applications."

"It wasn't a billion," I tease. "More like just a million."

"God, you must feel so relieved to not be on the hunt anymore. So, what is it? Spill!"

"You're looking at the newest junior editor at Room Publishing," I announce proudly.

"Junior editor? That's awesome! Isn't that what you were doing at McGregor?" Jen says.

"Yeah! I guess once you have even a little experience at a publishing company, it makes them more likely to hire you. I actually applied there before McGregor, even."

"That's so great! So maybe, this is where you were really supposed to end up all along!"

"Yeah, maybe!" I agree cheerfully. "I'm just happy to have a job at all. And I'm really, really glad I don't have to go back to waitressing or anything like that. It would be such a bummer after working in my field and actually using my degree, you know?"

"Totally," says Jen before ordering another round of drinks. Our first ones disappeared quickly, and I know we are in for a fun night.

"What do you know about the place? Do you like your new boss?"

"I don't actually know yet," I confess. "I know I like the kind of work they publish. I've read tons of their books. And their building is even nicer than McGregor's, so they must pull in a lot of clients and make good money. I think maybe I'll be working under the woman who interviewed me, and she seemed nice enough. But I'm not sure because she mentioned a few times that the owner should have been there for the interview, so maybe I'll be working directly for him? I'm not really sure how they operate there yet."

"I'm sure it'll be like McGregor but even better! And you'll be doing a similar job to what you were just doing, so you'll get the hang of it super quickly."

"I guess," I say, feeling a little wistful. "It just kind of sucks that I put so much energy and effort into McGregor, you know?" It was true. As my first real job, I put my heart and soul into my work there. I arrived early and left late every single day. I took on projects that nobody else wanted and always looked for opportunities to do more. I wanted to stand out, to impress. I wanted to move up the ladder quickly by working hard and learning everything I could about the company.

"Yeah," says Jen sympathetically, reaching over to give my hand a quick squeeze. "But it's not like that was exactly wasted time, was it? I mean, you got the work experience you needed to land the job at this new place. And I bet they called for a recommendation and heard nothing but wonderful things about you."

"That's probably true," I agreed, picturing floppy Brett singing my praises to Greta over the phone. Despite running out that day I got the notice I'd been laid off, Brett and I parted on great terms. When I went back into the office to collect my things, he asked to take me out for coffee, where he explained that he had wanted to tell me in person but couldn't get to me in time. He said McGregor had just lost a ton of money, some bad financial decisions had been made, and a bunch of people were laid off. I wasn't even the only junior editor in his department to go, and since I was such a new hire, there was no way he could save me from the chopping block, he'd said. But he did promise me a glowing letter of recommendation and told me to put him down as a reference to call him if I needed anything.

I would really miss working for him.

But maybe the people at Room Publishing would be just as kind and friendly.

After chatting a bit about Jen's work, I see her eyes start to scan the room over her drink.

"Uh oh," I grin. "I know that look."

"What?" Jen asks innocently, widening her eyes.

"See anyone cute?" I ask. I know she's checking out the guys here. More than one looked us over appreciatively when we walked up to the bar.

"No, no, we're here to celebrate you!"

"And we are!" I laugh. "Doesn't mean you can't talk to anyone else, though."

A cute guy who appears to be around our age approaches us.

"Excuse me, ladies," he says, smiling. "But my friend and I couldn't help but notice you. Is it alright if we buy you a drink?" he gestures to a table behind him, where another, equally cute guy is sitting.

Jen and I exchange glances, and without words, communicate to each other that it's okay.

"You know what? How about we join you?" Jen offers, spinning around on the stool and making her way over to the table, with me following quickly behind.

Several drinks, laughs, and dances later, Jen and I are stumbling out of the club and back into a cab. We giggle the whole way home, gushing about how hot and funny the guys were. When we get to our building, Jen gives me a big hug and congratulates me again before tripping up to her own apartment.

I quickly make some toast, still hungry from skipping dinner earlier. I set a tall glass of ice water on the bedside table, then wash my face, brush my teeth, and collapse into bed. When I sit up to gulp down some water, I notice the notepad where I wrote down notes from Greta earlier and smile to myself.

I can't wait to start my new job.

4
____

JOHN

"Juliette is leaving," says Greta, looking over her notes on her tablet resting on my desk in front of her. She's sitting across from me as we have coffee together, going over our schedules for the week.

"Oh, no," I say genuinely. "I'm sorry to hear that. Is everything okay?"

"Yes. Her husband got a job out west near both of their families, and she wants to have a baby soon and stay home for a few years."

"Well, good for her," I say, but I am sorry to see Juliette go. We hired her not very long ago, just within the past year, but she's been a great junior editor. "Let's be sure to get her a going away present, maybe have a staff party or something."

Even though it's a large company, I pride myself on knowing every single staff member personally. For example, I know Juliette got married just before accepting this job, and that her husband is an engineer. She's a hard worker and will be difficult to replace.

"Yes, I arranged a gift and sent out an email invitation for an office gathering at the end of this week," says Greta, as efficient as always.

"Great," I say, smiling across the desk at her, but she's still looking down at her notes.

"This means we will need to replace her, and as quickly as possible. She's got a full workload and we will need to reassign her clients right away."

"Right," I agree, nodding.

"I already posted the job, and cross-referenced new applicants with people who have applied before. I think we should pick someone who wants to work here badly enough to apply more than once, don't you think?"

"Great idea," I say, impressed. I didn't even know you could do that.

"I thought you'd say that," Greta smiles, tapping on her tablet with rapid fingers. "I already compiled a list of multiple-time applicants and emailed you their resumes. I think a few of them have great potential. I highlighted and added notes to some of them. All I need you to do is look them over and tell me which ones you want to bring in for an interview. With any luck, we can fill the position this week and have the new hire start first thing on Monday."

"Greta, you're incredible," I sigh. "What would I do without you?"

Greta is a tall, brassy blonde. She's probably in her late forties, although of course I'd never dare to ask. She has a witty, dry sense of humor and is sharp as a whip. She's worked in publishing since she graduated college and has been more of a mentor to me than an employee.

"Remember that when you're buying office Christmas gifts this year," she says with a wink. "Oh, wait, I do that, too."

"Well, get yourself something really nice," I laugh. "Is there anything else?"

"That's the last item on my list," Greta says, glancing at her notes one more time.

"Alright, I'll take a look at the resumes and let you know right away. Thanks, Greta."

"You're welcome," says Greta, rising from the chair and leaving the room.

As soon as the door closes behind her, I open up my email. I see one from Greta with the subject line "Junior Editor Candidates" right at the top of my inbox. I open the attachment with all the resumes and chuckle to myself at Greta's meticulous notes. She is truly invaluable. As much as I'm sorry to see Juliette go, losing Greta would be completely devastating. I make the big decisions, but she's really the one who runs this place on the day-to-day level. And I make sure her salary reflects that.

I skim through the pages and pages of resumes until I see something that makes my heart stop.

Lucy Myers.

That's the name at the top of one of the resumes.

It couldn't be.

Could it?

My heart pounding, I hit print on my computer and wait for the machine to put the resume on paper. As the printer whirs into action, I take deep breaths.

The resume slides out of the printer and falls neatly onto the tray below. The piece of paper taunts me, looking up at me mockingly. I snatch it out of the tray and pace around my office while I read it.

It definitely says Lucy Myers.

The same high school I went to is listed under the education section of her resume.

It's her. It's really her.

Clutching the paper in one hand and running my fingers through my hair wildly with the other, I continue to pace around my office while I hungrily take in the details of her resume.

She studied English in college and graduated with honors. Of course she did.

She was working for McGregor Publishing, a rival publishing company just a few short blocks from here. It doesn't look like she worked there very long, but there are no gaps in her resume, so there must be a good reason. I had heard rumblings of financial troubles at McGregor; maybe they had to let a few people go.

I can't believe it.

I've thought of Lucy Myers a million times since high school. In fact, she is one of the people — okay, probably the main person —

who helped me see that I was on the wrong path and needed to be a better guy.

She saw through all the bullshit — the jock exterior, the accolades, the bullying, all of it. She saw the real me. She knew I could be better; she knew I *was* better.

It crushed me when she turned me down at the end of my senior year. I never wanted to be with a girl as much as I wanted Lucy.

And to be honest, I'm not sure if I've ever felt that way about anyone else. Not even Olivia.

Lucy was different from anyone else in our school. She always stood out to me. Scenes from high school flash through my mind. Lucy in the cafeteria, dripping wet with a soda I dumped on her, looking furious and like she was about to cry. Lucy walking out of the prom after watching me dance with someone else. Lucy's sad eyes after I finally, finally worked up the nerve to kiss her.

Lucy telling me we couldn't be together, because I'd treated her so poorly.

Not that I can blame her.

God, I was such an idiot. An idiot and a jerk. I would never, ever treat any woman that way now, and I haven't since Lucy taught me that lesson.

I picture Bella now. I imagine some boy dumping a soda on her head, humiliating her in public, at a new school. My chest tightens. *I would murder that kid*, I think.

I don't know what to do.

I can't just ignore this. This is too big of a coincidence. What are the odds that, all these years later, Lucy Myers of all people would apply to work at my company?

Then I wonder if she has any idea that it's my company.

It wouldn't be hard to figure out. If she Googled my name, photos of me with various authors I've worked with over the years would pop up. But if she only researched the company, she probably has no clue, unless she ran across my name somewhere on the website.

Should I just call her? Dial the number on her resume?

And what? Apologize for being such a dick to her in high school? Offer her a job to make up for it?

It's not like she needs a pity hire. Her resume is very impressive. She's the candidate I would choose to interview even if I didn't know her.

My mind is reeling. I sit back down at my desk and bury my head in my hands.

I take some time to think and collect myself before making a decision. Finally, I summon Greta back into my office.

"Yes?" Greta says, standing in the doorway. I cross the room to meet her, handing her Lucy's resume.

"This one," I say definitively. "Call this one. Have her come in for an interview as soon as possible. Today, even. I mean, if she's available," I stutter.

"Okay," says Greta, giving me a look. I know I'm acting strangely, but Lucy Myers has always had that effect on me. "Do you have a certain day or time in mind?"

"You know what? Why don't you take this interview on your own," I say, and Greta looks at me like I've lost my mind.

"Are you okay?" she asks. "I mean — I'm sorry, it's just, I know you are particular about who you hire and you always sit in on interviews. Are you sure you want me to do this one alone?"

"One hundred percent sure. I trust your judgment, and I'm swamped this week. And, like you said, we've got to get someone to take over Juliette's workload quickly, right?"

"Yes," says Greta, still eying me suspiciously. "Okay, I'll call this—" she peers down at the resume in her hand, "Lucy Myers, right away. Did you find anyone else you want me to reach out to? There were lots of qualified candidates in that email."

"Ah, no, just this one for now."

"But if we need the position filled soon then—"

"I've got a good feeling about this one, Greta. Call it a hunch," I say, and again she looks at me like I've gone insane. I've got to get her out of my office before I blurt out anything stupid. "Thanks, Greta."

"You're welcome," she says slowly, keeping her eyes on me as she leaves the room again.

When she's gone, I collapse back in my desk chair and swivel to face the street. I look back down at all the people rushing to and fro. I can't believe, after all these years, that Lucy Myers was working just a few blocks away from me, living in the same city and breathing the same air, day after day. I peer down at the tiny figures below and wonder if one of them is Lucy. It could be.

Lucy Myers. I wonder what she's like now, after all this time.

She kept her last name, so she's not married. But lots of women keep their last names when they get married these days, and even if she's not married, it doesn't mean she's single.

Not that it matters. I don't know why I'm even thinking that way.

I wonder if she has even given me a thought since high school.

I wonder if she even remembers me.

5

LUCY

John McQueen.

I stare at the name on my computer screen in disbelief, an unpleasant rush of adrenaline flooding my system.

It can't be.

There's no way this could be the same John McQueen from high school. Could it?

It's Sunday night, the day before I'm supposed to start my new job at Room Publishing. Greta has already emailed me a couple of times this week with some onboarding instructions, but this is a letter from the CEO welcoming me to the company.

The CEO who I didn't get to meet when I went in for my interview last week.

I wring my hands, trying to calm down. I'm sitting in bed and was about to wind down for the evening when I decided to check my email one more time, just in case Greta had any last-minute details for me.

I nearly had a heart attack when I saw his name at the top of my inbox, attached to a Room Publishing Company email address.

I'm being ridiculous. John is like, maybe the most common name for man, ever. And McQueen is really common, too. I bet there are a million John McQueens out there. There's no way this is the same one I went to high school with.

But what if it is?

I could Google it and find out quickly. But then, even if it isn't the same John McQueen, I know myself and that I would stay up all night surfing the Web. I'd be exhausted and unprepared for my first day of work.

And if it *is* him...

No. It doesn't matter. It's not. It can't be.

John McQueen is... or at least was... a jock. And a jerk.

But he wasn't a total jerk.

Deep down, he was actually a really sweet, smart guy. He just let all the high school drama get to him.

But I highly doubt he grew up to be head of a publishing company. The John I knew was more likely to be a football player or a coach.

Guys in publishing are like my old boss, Brett. Kind, caring, sincere. Not like John, the boy who broke my heart in high school.

I snuggle under the covers and turn off the lamp. I fall into a restless sleep filled with troubling dreams. In the dreams, I'm sitting in the high school cafeteria holding a comically large cup of soda. It's the size of a trash can. I look down into the soda and see John McQueen. He looks trapped underneath the surface of the liquid, as if it's frozen over. He keeps opening his mouth, trying to tell me something, but I can't understand him.

I wake up and prepare for my first day of work, feeling unsettled.

I try to shake it off and treat myself to a coffee from the corner deli on my way into the new office. When I arrive, I take the elevator up to the correct floor and meet Greta in her office, just as she instructed me over email.

"Lucy!" She greets me with a smile. "Welcome aboard! I'm so glad you're here. Shall we go for a tour?"

Greta leads me around the office, showing me where everything is and introducing me to all of my new coworkers. I'm feeling a little overwhelmed, but it's similar to my first day at McGregor. At least I knew what to expect this time. I'm confident I can handle whatever they throw at me.

Greta leads me to a cubicle that's twice the size of my space at McGregor, and with much nicer equipment. The computer on the desk looks brand new, as does the comfortable-looking office chair.

"This will be your workspace," says Greta, gesturing to the cubicle. "I'm sorry about the workload." We both glance over at a massive stack of papers at the end of the desk. "But Juliette left unexpectedly and was in the middle of several projects. Today or perhaps later this week, we'll go through them together and decide how much you're comfortable taking on and redistribute the rest to other members of the team. How does that sound?"

"Perfect!" I agree, even though I already know that I will take on the entire pile. I am determined to work as hard here as I did at McGregor, and not to let that experience discourage me. I'm grateful to be a junior editor, but I don't want to be one forever. The harder I work, the faster I can learn the ropes and move up within the company.

"So, do you have any questions? I'll let you get settled in here, and then you can go down to HR to get your ID and all that settled. Oh, wait!" Greta says suddenly. "You haven't met John yet! I forgot that he was busy last week and couldn't meet you at your interview."

"Um... yeah," I reply nervously. In all the rushing around and taking in my new surroundings, I'd managed to forget about John McQueen. But now my nerves were resurfacing.

It's not him, it's not him, it's not him, I repeat to myself like a mantra, as Greta leads me to the office right next to hers. And I truly believe it — the world couldn't possibly be that small. John McQueen of Room Publishing has to be a sweet old bald man with liver spots and coffee breath, not a football jock from my high school. That would be ridiculous.

I take a deep breath as Greta raps her knuckles a couple of times on the door before opening it. We step inside together and...

Oh, my God.

I can't believe it.

It *is* him.

Seeing his face after all this time is like a punch to the gut. I feel like the wind has been knocked out of me. I can't breathe. I stand just inside the doorway dumbly, staring at him with my mouth hanging open.

I knew from the name on the email that there was a slim chance of this. I just didn't think it was really possible.

Greta, unaware of my inner turmoil, cheerily announces, "Lucy, I'd like you to meet John McQueen, CEO and owner of Room Publishing. John, this is our new junior editor, Lucy."

John's blue eyes bore into mine for a moment before he strides out from behind his desk and extends his hand toward me.

"Hello, Lucy," he says quietly.

Afraid I'm going to faint, I reach out my hand and grab onto his like it's a lifeline. As his warm palm presses against mine, a weird, not altogether unpleasant sensation takes over my body. It's a feeling I haven't experienced since high school –

unadulterated lust mixed with trepidation and anxiety.

"H…hi," I stutter, my voice cracking as our handshake lingers for a beat too long.

I'm both relieved and frustrated that Greta is here in the room with us. I'm not sure how to behave. Should I acknowledge that I recognize him? Pretend we've never met? I'm not comfortable being dishonest, but I'm not comfortable in any way right now.

Sensing my discomfort, or perhaps reading my mind with his penetrating gaze, John turns to Greta. "Greta, would you mind taking these —" He grabs a stack of envelopes from his desk and passes them to Greta. "Down to the mailroom? And Lucy, could you stay here please? I have a few quick things to go over with you, if you don't mind."

"Sure," Greta replies, her eyes darting back and forth between John and me suspiciously. She opens her mouth as if she's about to say something, then seems to think better of it and steps out of the office with the envelopes, closing the door behind her.

Now it's just John and me, alone in the room together.

"Do you want to sit down?" John asks.

I wordlessly sink into the chair across from him at his desk as he returns to his own seat.

"So, it's been a while, huh?" John smiles broadly.

I just stare at him, drinking him in.

I have to admit, he looks good. Great, really. He was always fit, but I knew him as a boy. Now he's a man and has really grown into his body. His expensive-looking suit frames his athletic figure well, the crisp seams emphasizing his broad shoulders. The blue of his tie makes his eyes pop. His blonde hair is thick, full and well-coiffed. He looks like he should be an underwear model, not the head of a publishing company.

I become acutely aware of my own appearance. Since it's the first day of a new job, I dressed carefully in a conservative navy skirt suit. I even wore tights and heels and put on a little bit of makeup — just mascara and some lipstick. I feel like a flight attendant, but Jen helped me pick this suit out, promising that it was chic, and she would certainly know better than I would.

Not that it matters what I look like, I think to myself fiercely. But after... God, how long has it been? Ten years? Twelve? After that much time has passed, you wonder how someone else sees you. If you look better, worse, or the same as you did before.

I realize suddenly that John doesn't look at all surprised to see me, nor does he seem to be studying my appearance the same way I'm studying his.

"Did you — did you know it was me when you hired me?" I ask dumbly. John smiles, the corners of his eyes crinkling with mirth.

"Lucy, of course I knew it was you! I have to tell you, I was..." here he pauses, as if searching for the right word, "*delighted* when I saw your resume. From your reaction, I'm guessing you had no idea that I'm affiliated with Room Publishing?"

It's kind of nice that he says "affiliated," I note. It would be an easy opportunity for him to brag about being the owner and CEO, but he's more humble than that. Interesting.

"No, I had no idea," I say softly. "I mean, I got an email from you yesterday and saw your name, but I thought, you know, there's no way…"

"Yeah, I guess this isn't exactly where you'd guessed I'd end up, huh?" John grimaces.

"Not really," I admit.

"Don't tell anyone, but I've always loved English," says John with a wink that makes me go a little weak in the knees. I'm glad I'm already sitting down.

"I guess so," I say.

"What, you expected me to be an athlete or something still?" he jokes, and I am taken right back to high school. I can feel the soda dripping down the back of my neck after he threw it on me in the cafeteria.

"Actually, I didn't expect anything about you at all," I snap before I can stop myself. Because really, who does he think he is? Does he really assume I've been thinking about him at all? That I've been pining away for him, imagining what his life is like now?

If I'm being honest, I *have* given John McQueen more than a passing thought over the years, and I *have* wondered where he ended up. But it's so typical for him to just assume that everyone is obsessed with him and preoccupied with what he's doing. And judging by how successful his business appears to be, he's probably even more self-satisfied than he was back then.

John looks at me like I've slapped him, and I think, *oh shit*. He may be an arrogant jerk, but he's still my boss. My brand new boss, and I was just rude to him.

"Okay, okay, fair enough," John jokes, raising his hands in surrender. "I guess I deserve that. But I will say, Lucy, I've definitely thought about you."

"Is that why you hired me? Because you were curious? Or, like, wanted to mess with me?" I ask haughtily, a flush creeping up my cheeks. I know I should have better self-control, but I can't seem to stop myself.

"No, no! It's not like that at all!" John says so insistently that I believe him. "I needed a new junior editor, and you made the short-list before I even got involved with the decision-making process. Your resume is very impressive, Lucy. You should be proud."

"Thanks," I respond automatically, in spite of myself.

"I hired you based on your merit, and it was just a bonus that I happen to already know you, I swear."

We're both quiet for a moment and I'm deciding how to respond, when something occurs to me.

"How come you didn't tell me it was you? Like, in your welcome letter? Or why weren't you at my interview?"

"I had a scheduling conflict," John replies smoothly, his eyes flickering down towards his desk as he speaks. "And the interview was more of a formality; I already knew, based on your resume and what I know of your character that you were the perfect fit."

"How do you know anything about my character?" I ask incredulously. "For all you know, I could have become a convicted felon after high school!"

At this, John bursts out laughing. "You? A criminal? Never!"

"Okay, maybe not," I smile reluctantly. "But did you even run a background check on me?"

"I did the necessary research that I would do on any prospective hire," John says evenly, and he does that thing where he looks down again. Is he lying? But why?

"And what about the letter? You could have said who you were then," I point out.

"That's just a form letter I send to all new hires. It's just a copy and paste job. And my name is on it, so I figured if you didn't already know I worked here, that would tell you. You didn't look me up, even after getting that email?"

"No, I didn't," I admit, looking down at my hands in my lap. "I just thought maybe it was a common name. And, like you said, I didn't exactly expect you to end up in a place like this."

"Do you have any more questions for me?" He gives me a pointed look, and I feel embarrassed by my rude line of questioning.

"I'm sorry, it's just a little weird, seeing you after all this time," I confess.

"I understand, but I hope you don't think I hired you for any reason other than your skills and experience. And I'm happy that you're here, Lucy. I really am. I think you're going to fit in well, and Room is lucky to have you. I—" he looks away, coughs, then continues, his voice filled with underlying meaning. "I'm lucky to have you, Lucy."

There he goes again with the intense eye contact. I feel his blue eyes penetrating mine, searching my face.

I break the moment by looking away, my gaze resting on his hands. That's when I notice he's not wearing a wedding ring. My stomach fills with butterflies against my will.

"Isn't it some sort of conflict of interest for me to be working for you? Since I knew you before? Like, couldn't that be something we could get in trouble for?" I ask.

"If it's not a problem for you, then it's not a problem for me," says John, leaning back in his chair. Then I remember that he is the owner and CEO, after all. Ultimately, he makes the rules.

"Can I ask just one thing?" I say.

"Anything," John replies, leaning forward again.

"Can we just... act like we don't know each other?"

John looks surprised, then hurt, so I hurriedly add, "Just because I don't want anyone to think I'm getting preferential treatment or anything like that. I would hate for anyone here to have a reason to dislike me before they even get to know me."

"I can understand that," John nods. "Sure, if that will make you more comfortable."

"Okay then," I say, standing up and smoothing down my skirt. "Is there anything else?"

"Not at the moment, no. Thank you, Lucy. And again... I'm really glad you're here."

I want to reply, "Me, too," but can't quite bring myself to say it. I simply leave his office, closing the door silently behind me.

6

JOHN

In the days after I saw Lucy's application, my mind was completely consumed by her.

She came into the office for an interview the day after Greta called her. I knew when she was coming because Greta scheduled it in our shared digital calendar. "Lucy Myers interview – 1:00 pm." The letters on the calendar glared at me from my screen as the clock counted down to her arrival.

I made sure that Greta believed I was on a conference call at that time so she wouldn't come see me for any reason. Just to be on the safe side, though, I locked my office door, something I rarely do.

It's not that I didn't want to see Lucy. I was actually really looking forward to it. I just thought if she saw me at the interview, it might scare her off. We didn't exactly part on the best of terms all those years ago, and I would have hated for her to turn down the job just because she was so surprised, or even angry, to see me.

I knew she needed this job. I had Greta run a traditional background check, just like I would for any new employee. But I wanted to know more about what Lucy had been up to since high school.

It was okay these days for bosses to look up prospective hires on the Internet, right? It was perfectly normal, even expected. It would be stranger if I *didn't* do a little digging into Lucy's history. At least, that's what I told myself as I opened a new browser window on my computer. Never mind the fact that I never bothered to look up any potential employees before.

I hesitated for only a second before my fingers typed out her name into the search engine. Thousands of results came up, and I weeded through the first couple of pages to find the right Lucy Myers. I found her LinkedIn page, which reflected what I already knew from her resume. I also found the website for the publication that she had co-founded. I skimmed through the website, impressed by the caliber of her work. Impressed, but unsurprised. Lucy was always smart and driven, and I was happy to see that hadn't changed.

I wondered if she had changed in other ways.

I clicked over to the images tab to see what I could find there. I scrolled through lots of pictures of random smiling women, none of them the Lucy Myers I was looking for. After scrolling through a few pages, a particular thumbnail caught my eye.

It was her.

Her face, in a thumbnail photo no larger than a postage stamp, peered out at me from the screen. I felt my breath catch in my throat at seeing her face after all these years.

I quickly double-clicked the thumbnail, enlarging the image. It was the profile picture for one of her personal social media pages. She was wearing a red dress and a matching red lip color. Her skin was tanned and freckled, and she wore a large, genuine smile on her face. Her hair was long, blonde, and glossy. Another person – a woman, judging from the hand wrapped around her waist – was cropped out of the photo.

She looked incredible, just like I remembered her. Better, even. We were only kids when I knew Lucy, and she was still growing into her body. She never knew how beautiful she was, seemingly uncomfortable with herself. In this photo, she was a woman who had fully stepped into her beauty and appeared comfortable in her own skin. The confidence that radiated off of her made her even more stunning.

Before I could stop myself, I clicked on the image, which took me to her Instagram page. Luckily her profile was public so I could see all of her photos.

I settled in and looked through more than 100 photos on her page, starting from the bottom, the oldest photos. There were lots of shots of Lucy and another girl I recognized from high school – Jennifer, I believe. The two of them graduating college, taking road trips together, or excitedly showing off their publication. There were pictures of Lucy on the beach in cutoff shorts and a tank top. Pictures of her with her parents. And most recently, pictures of her in her new apartment in Chicago. One caption referenced her job at McGregor, and the newest photo was of her painted toenails propped up in a bubble bath. The caption read "Self-care after a long day of job hunting" accompanied by a stressed-out emoji face.

I had also done some digging on McGregor Publishing and discovered that they had, in fact, suffered a huge financial blow and had to lay off employees. Lucy hadn't been working there for very long, so it made sense that they would let her go, even if she was a great employee. Greta had already checked her references and they had nothing but wonderful things to say about Lucy, which was unsurprising. At least, I thought, I could honorably defend my decision to hire her. She really was the best candidate for the position, and I would have picked her even without knowing who she was.

Lucy's Instagram led me to her Facebook and then to her Twitter profile, where I found more evidence of her distress over losing her job. *Poor Lucy*, I thought. It looked like she had just moved to Chicago around the same time she started working for McGregor Publishing. It was only a few months ago and she must have been devastated to lose her job so quickly.

Well, that settled it. Lucy needed a job, and I needed a junior editor. And, to be honest, I really wanted to see Lucy Myers again.

But I had to restrain myself and wait until she accepted the job. I didn't want her memories of me to sour her against working here. By the time she figured out who I was, she could decide for herself if she wanted to stay. Knowing how badly she needed the work, though, I doubted she would be able to walk away, no matter how she felt about me. That is, if she even felt anything at all.

What if she didn't even remember me? I know Lucy left a huge impression on me and changed who I was as a person. But I had no reason to think that I had done the same for her in any way.

Or did she know that I owned Room Publishing? Could she possibly have applied here *because* of me? To improve her odds of getting the job based on a personal connection... or for another reason?

That was unlikely, I decided, feeling only slightly disappointed. Coming from McGregor, she likely just applied to all similar publishing houses in the area. It's what I would have done in her shoes.

At the time of Lucy's interview, it took all the restraint I had in me to wait in my office. I watched the clock and heard Greta's office door open next to mine right at 1:00 p.m. My heart pounded as I heard my assistant's heels clicking as she walked away, most likely to meet Lucy in the lobby.

A couple of minutes passed, which felt like hours. Even though I'd locked the door, I closed out of the browsers where I had Lucy's social media profiles pulled up, guilty for having them open while she was in the building. Then I heard two sets of footsteps approach Greta's door – the familiar click of Greta's heels and slightly softer steps of someone else.

Lucy.

I could hear their muffled voices in the hallway, although I couldn't make out the words. The door opened and closed again, and I knew the interview had begun.

The walls between mine and Greta's offices were thick, so I couldn't hear a thing. It was wild knowing that Lucy Myers was in the room right next to me, just a few feet away.

After a few attempts to concentrate on some work, I gave up and just sat back in my chair, reminiscing. Finally, after nearly an hour, I heard Greta's door open again and the two sets of footsteps walking away.

When Greta returned, I was standing in my doorway waiting for her.

"So? How did it go?" I asked, trying to sound casual.

"Great!" Greta replied brightly. "I think she'll fit in wonderfully here!"

"Good," I said, breathing a sigh of relief. If Lucy had bombed the interview, it would have been a lot harder justifying hiring her, both to myself and to Greta.

"Are you sure you don't want me to interview anyone else? I think she's the right choice, but there are so many other good candidates out there..."

"No, there's no need to spend any more time on this," I said firmly. "If you felt good about the interview, you can go ahead and offer her the job."

"You're the boss!" Greta said, heading back into her office.

Now it's Monday, and I finally got to see Lucy face to face. Judging from her reaction, she was genuinely surprised to see me. So much for any thoughts that she may applied here because of me, even though I knew that wasn't the case.

After our somewhat awkward, tense meeting in my office, I lean back in my chair determining how to handle everything. Lucy doesn't want anyone in the office to know about our history together. I can respect that, but it does complicate things a little.

I owe Lucy at least this much. If her social media is any indicator, she needs this job. I don't want her to feel uncomfortable with me or in any way at work. I promise myself that I'll make her work environment as safe and enjoyable as possible. For now, I'll treat her just like any other employee, even if I just can't see her that way.

Who knows, maybe one day we can be friends again?

7

———

LUCY

Life has a funny way of working out sometimes.

I landed my dream job, in my dream city, with my dream apartment, only to lose my job quickly. Then I land my dream job again, only to find out that John McQueen, of all people, is my new boss.

The first couple of days of work were uncomfortable, to say the least. Even though my cubicle isn't within sight of John's office, I found myself hyper-aware of how I was sitting, what I was wearing, and even how loudly I was breathing. It was a huge challenge to meet all my new coworkers and try to make a good impression, or get any work done, all while thinking John could be watching me at any time.

Not that I care what John thinks of me. I don't.

But he is my new boss, and on top of that he's somebody I didn't leave on the best of terms.

And, fine, I'll admit, he's still one of the best-looking guys I've ever seen.

It's the perfect cocktail for nerves and anxiety.

But toward the end of the week, I start to relax a little. I've noticed that John rarely comes out of his office, and when he does, he keeps his promise to treat me just like any other employee. Looking in from the outside, you would never know that this was the guy who bullied me in high school. The same guy who later wanted to date me, before I turned him down.

Now I can almost forget that he's working just a few steps away from me. Out of everyone in the office, I interact mostly with the other junior editors and Greta. It's actually a lot like McGregor, and the familiarity is comforting.

I'm sitting at my desk drafting an email to one of the clients I took over from my predecessor when my personal email, open in another browser window, pings with a new message alert.

I click over to view the message and see it's from my bank, immediately setting my nerves on edge.

Because when is news from the bank ever *good* news? It's not like it'll ever be a notification that a ton of money has magically appeared in my account.

I open the email, bracing myself for an overdraft fee.

As I skim the email, I feel a nervous flush creep up my cheeks. It's not quite as bad as I expected, but it's not great either. It's a notification of low funds.

Immediately after that, my email pings again.

It's an automated reminder from my apartment manager that rent is due soon.

My eyes flicker back and forth between the two open emails. The number remaining in my bank account is less than what I owe for rent.

My anxiety spikes as I realize that I won't be getting my first paycheck from Room Publishing until the end of next week, which is after rent is due.

Shit.

I feel a lump in my throat and my eyes watering, and know I have to get out of here quickly before I burst into tears and make a scene.

I stand up from my desk and walk briskly to the restroom, struggling to keep it together before pushing open a stall door and locking myself inside. I peek underneath the surrounding stalls, checking for feet to make sure I'm alone. Then I let the tears fall freely.

I sob, thinking about what I can possibly do about the situation. I didn't have much in savings, but that account is now drained because I had to pay bills after losing my job at McGregor. Rent is due, and as a newer tenant I really, really don't want to have to ask for an extension. Plus, knowing how competitive the housing market is where I live, I doubt the building owners would give me one anyway. I've never met them; they don't live in town. Jen and I both just mail off our rent checks every month. They don't know me personally and have no reason to make an exception for me.

As my tears start to slow, I breathe deeply and think about what Jen would do. When I lost my job at McGregor Publishing, she said she could help me out with rent money, but I know she's in no better shape financially than I am. If she has any money to lend me, she'd have to pull it out of her savings. And what if she needs that money soon, before I can repay her? I know she'd give it to me without hesitation, but I really don't want to have to ask her for that.

I could always ask my parents for money, but I'm reluctant. I know they would help me out, but they've already done so much for me. They were so proud and happy for me when I moved into my apartment here and got my first publishing job. I don't want to worry or disappoint them.

Plus, there's the small matter of the fact that I didn't tell them about losing my job at McGregor.

I should have, but I was so hopeful that I'd find another job quickly and never have to tell them about being laid off. I figured eventually, once I was settled in at a new position, I'd casually mention that I transitioned to another company.

So, although I could probably get the money I need, my stomach churns at the thought of asking Jen or my parents for it.

I realize I've been in the bathroom for far too long. Someone might notice I've been away from my desk and sitting here crying isn't going to solve anything.

I open the stall door and examine myself in the mirror. My mascara is running, and my nose and cheeks are bright red. Impatiently, I splash some cold water from the sink on my face and dab a paper towel underneath my eyes to clean up smeared makeup. I'm still blotchy, but maybe no one will notice. I can just say it's allergies.

I take one more breath, shake out my hair, and open the bathroom door.

And run right into someone.

I slam against someone's chest with such force that I start to fall backward before strong hands grab my waist, keeping me from toppling over completely.

Embarrassed, I glance up and realize that the hands – and the chest – belong to John.

Of course, I would run into him like this. I've successfully avoided him all week, for the most part. And now he's catching me at the worst possible time.

If he asks me what's wrong, I might burst into tears again, so I try to keep my head down to hide my face.

"Lucy!" he says, surprised, as though he forgot I even work here.

"Sorry, I'm so clumsy," I mumble.

"Yeah, I remember that about you," John jokes, not unkindly. His hands are still on my waist, but he clears his throat and drops them quickly. For a second, I weirdly wish he would keep holding me, but I immediately shake the thought away.

He glances around furtively to make sure no one heard the comment. "Sorry," he adds, seemingly apologizing for the familiarity.

"It's fine," I say, and try to walk away.

"Hang on." John peers into my face, forcing me to make eye contact. "Are you okay?"

At the sound of the genuine concern in his voice, I feel tears welling up again.

Dammit.

"It's nothing," I say, but my voice catches in my throat.

"It's not nothing. What's wrong? Are you sick? Do you need to take the day off?"

"No, no, nothing like that," I say quickly, not wanting to lose a day's pay.

"Is the workload too much? I told Greta we shouldn't have let you take over all of Juliette's work. It's way too much at the start of a new job," John says, frustrated.

"No, the work is fine," I say truthfully. It *is* a lot of work, but it's nothing I can't handle. And I need to stay as distracted with as much work as possible so that I don't worry about seeing John all the time.

"Then what is it?" John's eyes cloud over with anger. "Is someone... did someone say something rude to you? Are you being harassed? Because I can promise you, I will *not* tolerate it in my office!" He sounds so earnest and I can't help but allow a giggle to escape through my tears.

"No, no, I swear, it's nothing like that."

John eyes me for a moment as if weighing a decision in his mind, then says, "Well, you're in no shape to go back to work. I was just about to step out for a coffee, why don't you join me?"

"Oh no, I couldn't..." I protest. "Really, I'm fine, I'll just go back to my desk."

"I insist."

I have to agree. His tone is firm and he is my boss, after all. Plus, a hot cup of coffee sounds nice right now.

As we head to the lobby, I think if anyone would have told me back in high school that in the future I'd be going out for coffee with John McQueen, my boss, I would have said they were crazy.

Like I said, life has a funny way of working out sometimes.

8

____

JOHN

I'm heading toward the elevator, wanting some fresh air and a cup of coffee. I've already had my coffee from Greta today, but work is insane. I need a break and another dose of caffeine to get through the day.

Apparently, someone else at work is having as crazy of a day as I am.

As I pass the restrooms on my way out, a small figure comes flying out of the ladies' room. Whoever it is bounces off me, almost comically, and starts to fall.

Reflexively, I grab whoever it is to help keep them upright.

That's when I realize who it is.

"Lucy!" I exclaim in surprise.

When I see her face, it's like a blast from the past. I'm transported back to high school, to another time when Lucy ran into me outside of a restroom.

I see her blotchy little face, and instead of a woman, I see the teenage girl she used to be. The one who I dumped soda on until she fled to the bathroom in tears.

The guilt hits me hard, like a punch in the stomach. I wonder, ashamed, if Lucy still remembers that day… if she still thinks about it ever.

I can't change what I did in the past, but I can try to fix whatever is wrong now.

Lucy mumbles an apology, something about being clumsy, and I can't help but laugh to myself. She *was* always kind of a klutz, but on her it was charming.

I realize my hands have lingered on her waist for too long, and I abruptly pull away. My fingers feel warm from where they were pressed against her.

She's obviously been crying but refuses to tell me what's wrong. I need to get to the bottom of this. I can't have her this upset at work. I promised myself that I would make sure she feels safe and comfortable here.

But I also need to get the hell out of this office for a few minutes and grab that coffee. I insist that Lucy joins me on my outing. Maybe the break will do her some good, and just maybe I can get her to open up about whatever is bothering her.

There's an awkward silence between us as we take the elevator down to the lobby. I don't want to make her feel uncomfortable, and I want to keep my promise to her, treating her like any other employee.

Even though she most certainly is not.

As we make our way through the lobby, I nervously attempt to make small talk.

"So, nice weather we've been having lately, huh?"

Lucy looks up at me as we walk and laughs.

"What?" I ask.

"Really? You want to talk about the weather?" She grins.

"No, not really," I reply honestly, grinning back. This is one of the things I remember admiring about Lucy; she's an honest, no bullshit type of person. I'm glad to see she's still the same way.

Plus, I'm glad I could make her smile.

The coffee shop is only a few doors down, on the same block. We get there before I can even strike up a new line of conversation.

There is no one in line, so we walk right up to the counter where a male barista is standing, ready to take our order.

"I'll have a coffee, black, and...?" I look over at Lucy questioningly.

"Oh, um, I'll... have the same," she says timidly. I can tell it's not what she really wants.

"Wait, I changed my mind," I say, scanning the menu board on the wall above the counter. "I'll have... a caramel macchiato instead, please. Don't you want to try something else, too, Lucy?"

"Um, actually, yeah," Lucy says, sounding braver and a little relieved. "Can I please have a vanilla latte instead?"

"And... we'll take a couple of blueberry muffins and croissants, please," I add finally. Lucy might be hungry, but I'm not sure what she'd want.

"Sure thing," the barista responds, giving Lucy an appreciative once over and ringing up our total. I glare at him, handing over my credit card and ignoring Lucy's protests.

"I invited you out to coffee, plus I'm the boss," I tease. "So, I pay."

"If you insist," she teases back.

We sit down across from each other at a low table and wait for our order.

"So, if we can't talk about the weather, is it okay if I ask you how your family has been?" I say. "Or is that too personal?"

"No, no, it's fine." Lucy appears embarrassed. "I'm sorry I asked you to act like you don't know me, I guess that's pretty rude. But you know how it can be sometimes. I wouldn't want any of the other editors to think I have an unfair advantage because I knew you before, or anything like that."

"I completely understand," I say, nodding in agreement. "It *is* kind of hard keeping secrets from Greta, though."

And I'm only partially kidding. Greta is my right-hand man, or rather, my right-hand woman. She has worked for me for years and knows all my quirks and habits. She was definitely suspicious when I had her interview Lucy on her own and didn't interview anyone else for Juliette's position. In addition to knowing me inside and out, she's smart as a whip, and there's no getting anything past her. It's what makes her such a fantastic employee.

"She's great." Lucy perks up at Greta's name.

"Isn't she?" I agree.

"She's so nice, and she's been super helpful in helping me take over the last editor's clients," Lucy prattles. Her hands are resting on the table, and she's twisting her fingers together nervously.

Am I making her nervous?

No, it's probably whatever was bothering her earlier, and I remind myself to get to the bottom of it. But first I have to get her to relax and open up a little.

"You can go ahead and tell her if you want," says Lucy suddenly. "In fact, forget what I said about pretending not to know me. Now that I've met everyone and settled in a little bit, they all seem really nice. I don't think anyone would care or hold it against me."

"Well, it's not like I'm going to announce it at a meeting or anything," I joke. "But I appreciate that. I've definitely learned that it's easier to be honest, in general."

"Have you?" Lucy's eyes catching mine for a second before she looks away.

"Yeah," I say, surprised. "Like, for example, I really do want to know how your family is doing. How is everyone? When did you move to Chicago?"

The barista sets our order down on the table, shooting Lucy a wink and a smile that she appears not to notice as she thanks him. I want to tell the guy off, but I restrain myself. What business is it of mine if he wants to flirt with Lucy? Still, the guy's got balls and for all he knows, I could be Lucy's boyfriend.

Lucy's looking at me, and it's almost like she can read my thoughts. I flush with embarrassment but try to cover it up by taking a sip of my sugary drink. It's way too sweet, but I'll choke it down for Lucy's sake.

Then she launches into answering my question, and the awkwardness is set aside as we catch up. We swap stories about our folks, then talk about our work history. Lucy fills me in on what she's been doing professionally for the last few years, most of which I already knew from her resume and her social media.

"That all sounds very impressive," I say sincerely as Lucy finishes telling me about the publication she started after college with her friend Jen. "And, like I told you, that's exactly why I hired you. You're very professional and driven."

"Thanks," says Lucy, looking down and blushing.

"So, what has someone like you so rattled back at the office?" I ask, hope she might be ready to tell me now.

"I don't want to say," Lucy answers softly. Again, I admire her honesty; most people would have just made up some excuse.

"You can tell me," I coax. "In fact, if anyone at the office is giving you trouble, I really need you to tell me."

"No, no, it's nothing like that. It's just embarrassing."

"What is it?" I press. "Work stuff? Friend trouble? Boyfriend drama?" I watch her face carefully for a reaction.

"No, that's not it." She sighs, and my heart jumps in my chest. So, maybe she's single, I think. That's interesting.

"Okay, so what is it then?"

"My rent is due and I'm completely broke," she blurts, looking mortified. "It's just... I used up my savings while I was unemployed, and I'd already spent so much money just to move here and get an apartment. And now rent is due, and I don't have it, and I don't want to ask my family for a bailout, and I won't get my first paycheck until it's too late."

"Oh," I answer, surprised. I wasn't expecting it to be money trouble, and I'm not quite sure what to say.

"Yeah. Totally embarrassing, right? I should have my finances more together, but I'm really just starting out on my career, and wasn't expecting to get laid off like that."

"It's not embarrassing, it's very understandable," I say, even though it's not that relatable to me. I've been fortunate to grow up with family money and ever since Room Publishing took off, let's just say I probably won't ever have to worry about finances.

It breaks my heart that someone as hardworking as Lucy is living paycheck-to-paycheck. She doesn't deserve that kind of stress.

A vision of Lucy as a teenager comes to me again, unbidden. I imagine her sad, mortified face, dripping with soda. She didn't deserve that, either.

I have to do something to help her.

She's picking at the muffin in front of her, miserably, when an idea comes to me.

"Did Greta ever mention that you get a sign-on bonus?" I say, trying to sound casual.

"What?" Lucy instantly abandons the muffin that she's picked to pieces and looks up sharply.

"Yeah, it's standard policy. You get a new hire sign-on bonus, effective immediately. You've already set up direct deposit with HR, right? It should be in your account by the end of the day."

I make a mental note to wire the money the second we return to the office.

I watch as a range of emotions crosses Lucy's face. First disbelief, then excitement, followed by relief. Then she's back to disbelief again, with a hint of suspicion.

"But... but I didn't see anything in my contract about..."

"It's kind of a new policy, they might not have updated the contract to reflect it yet," I lie.

It's so brand new, in fact, that I just made it up.

I see her process my words and start to believe them.

"Oh, my God, that's such a huge relief! How much is the bonus, if you don't mind my asking?"

I blurt out the first number that comes to mind that I think is reasonable, plus a little extra. This is Lucy, after all.

I resist the urge to laugh as her eyes widen and her jaw drops, creating three perfect circles on her face.

"That's insane!" she exclaims. "That's way too generous for a sign-on bonus!"

"I want employees to feel valued," I shrug. And it's true. I make another mental note to actually build a sign-on bonus into new hire contracts in the future.

"Wow," Lucy breathes, elated. "I can't believe it. That's amazing. Thank you."

"You're welcome, but really, it's just policy," I say, feeling guilty for lying but knowing she would never accept the money otherwise. I'm doing the right thing.

"Well, still. Thank you," Lucy says genuinely. "Not just for the bonus, but for bringing me here. For the coffee. For trying to make me feel better." She looks at me like she's staring at a bizarre piece of art that she can't quite interpret.

"Any time," I reply, and I mean it. I enjoy talking to Lucy, and this coffee break will probably be the highlight of my day, if not my entire week.

We finish our drinks and linger for a while, casually picking at our pastries, in no rush to head back to work.

Finally, Lucy glances at my watch and notices the time.

"We'd better get back," she says, shooting up out of her chair and sounding panicked. "I didn't realize we've been gone for so long."

"Relax," I laugh. "Who's going to get you in trouble? I'm the boss, remember?"

"I know, I know, but I really have a lot of work to do," she says, almost apologetic.

"Yeah, me too," I sigh, standing up with her. "Alright, let's go."

All too soon, we're back in the elevator headed up to the office.

"This was nice," Lucy says quietly, not making eye contact. "Thanks again."

"My pleasure. Maybe we'll do it again sometime. Not the running into each other part, but the coffee."

"Yeah," Lucy agrees. "That would be nice."

I watch her small frame walk towards her cubicle, her long blonde hair cascading down her back.

Then I return to my office, where I immediately transfer money into Lucy's account and email Greta about changing the new hire contract.

9

LUCY

"So, the money just miraculously showed up in your account today?" Jen says, expertly twirling noodles around a pair of plastic chopsticks. She's sitting on my couch while I sprawl across the floor in front of the television in my apartment, both of us eating the takeout I treated us to. I can afford it, with the insane bonus from Room Publishing.

I just finished telling Jen about my money troubles, running into John in the office, and having coffee with him. I told her how kind he was, how he seemed genuinely interested in my problems and what I had to say.

And I didn't say this part out loud, but actually it was better than most first dates I've been on recently. Not that it was a date, of course.

Of course not.

"Yeah, isn't that wild? I was so stressed out about rent, but look how perfectly everything worked out! I'm feeling really good about this job," I reply happily, digging into my own carton of food.

"Yeah, it's great," Jen says, but I can tell something is bothering her.

"What is it?"

"Oh, nothing."

"Come on, tell me!"

"Well," Jen sighs, "I'm glad you're happy at your new job and everything, and I don't want to sound negative... but don't you think that it's a little strange, the money just showing up like that?"

"John said it's a standard sign-on bonus for all new employees," I argue.

"But you said it's not in your contract?" Jen points out, raising an eyebrow.

"No..." I say. "But John said—"

"Companies don't just give employees money like that, especially when they're not contractually obligated," Jen interrupts. "And a big company like that wouldn't just *forget* to put something like that in a contract. Plus, the number you told me is *way* higher than any sort of sign-on bonus I've ever heard of. And you said no one mentioned it when they hired you?"

"No..." I admit, frustrated. "But John said—"

"John can say whatever he wants!" Jen explodes. "He owns the company; he could snap his fingers and have the contracts changed by tomorrow! He could also snap his fingers and have that money sent to you."

"But why would he do that?"

"I don't know, but I don't like it. I don't trust him," Jen tells me.

After my first day at Room, I'd told Jen everything about how John McQueen, the football star from our high school, was my new boss. She didn't like it. Her memories of John are even less fond than my own. But, like me, she figured this was a good job opportunity. I couldn't let some high school bully get in the way of doing what was best for me, even if that meant working for him.

"So what are you saying? You think he just... gave me the money?" I ask, trying to figure out the pieces of the puzzle. Jen is right, it *is* strange that the money showed up right after talking to John. And that it isn't in my contract, and no one throughout the hiring process ever mentioned anything about it. And it *is* a lot of money. A whole lot.

I'm starting to feel foolish, like I've been duped.

"But why on Earth would John lie about *giving* me money?" I ask Jen.

"Well, for one thing, would you have accepted it otherwise?" Jen retorts, already knowing my answer. "And, I don't know, maybe he wants something. Maybe he's going to hold it over your head and cash in when he needs you to do something for him."

"Like what?" I ask, and Jen wiggles her eyebrows at me suggestively. "Oh, gross! Stop it," I cry, reaching over to whack Jen with a throw pillow.

We chew our food in silence for a bit, pretending to watch the show on TV but both of us really lost in thought.

"Wait a second!" Jen says suddenly, snapping out of her reverie. "When you checked your bank account, did you notice where the money came from?"

"What do you mean?"

"You know, your account it shows where a deposit came from? Here, pull up your account. Can I see?"

Because she's my best friend and knows everything about me anyway, I pull up my bank account on my phone, tap in the password, and pass it over to Jen.

She scrolls and taps for a minute, then shouts, "Aha! I knew it!"

"What?" I climb up next to her on the couch, peering over her shoulder at the screen.

"See?" She points to the screen. "This is your deposit history. This is the amount you got as your bonus today, and this is where the bank says it came from."

I look at the words and numbers, still not getting it. "*Okay*? It says I have a big fat deposit from John McQueen. I'm confused, what are we looking at here?"

"Exactly!" Jen says triumphantly. "It's from *John McQueen*. Not from Room Publishing. Get it? I bet you anything when you get your paycheck next week the deposit will say Room Publishing, not your boss's name."

It all clicks together, and I'm at a loss for words.

"But I still don't understand *why*."

"I don't either, but I'd be careful if I were you," Jen warns.

"Do you think I should give the money back?" I ask anxiously.

"Hell no! You can't anyway, right? You just sent your rent, didn't you?"

"Yeah, well, maybe I should pay him back when I get my paycheck next week?"

"Does your paycheck even match that *bonus*?" Jen asks suspiciously, putting the word "bonus" in air quotes.

"Not even close," I admit, feeling really stupid now. "I'm such an idiot. Why didn't I see this?"

"Hey, look, don't feel bad." Jen squeezes my shoulder. "I'm sorry. I really didn't mean to bring you down. I'm super proud of you for getting a great new job so quickly, and it's awesome that you got a little extra money. I just don't trust this guy, and want you to be careful, that's all. It's probably not a big deal, but you should be aware of it, you know?"

"You're right," I sigh.

"Remember who he is. How he treated you back in high school."

"But don't you think people change?" I ask.

"Not that much," Jen says, pursing her lips.

That night, I lay in bed, tossing and turning furiously as I replay everything again in my mind. Having coffee with John. The money appearing in my account, solving all my problems. The deposit, clearly showing that the money came directly from John's personal bank account. Jen's warning about how people don't change is really making me think.

By morning, I'm exhausted, irritated, and more confused than ever.

I can't just pretend like I don't know about the money. I have to confront John about it. I don't know what I'll say, but I know I have to say *something*.

On my way into work, I pass the coffee shop John and I went to yesterday. For a second, I consider popping in to grab him a coffee to say thank you for his help yesterday. Then I remember that he's a liar and I'm upset with him, so I just keep walking briskly by the storefront.

I barrel into John's office, not even bothering to stop at my desk first to put down my purse. I fling the door open without knocking and open my mouth to barrage him with questions when I see something that halts me in my tracks. I freeze.

It's a little girl.

She looks to be just a little older than a toddler. She's sitting on the floor of John's office, surrounded by toys and coloring books. I take in her fair, curly hair and eyes the same shade of blue as John's.

I realize with a jolt that this must be his daughter.

He never mentioned having a daughter.

"Lucy!" John smiles, and for the first time I notice him sitting at his desk, typing away. He looks about as exhausted as I feel, but still happy to see me.

"Lucy!" mimics the little girl on the carpet, standing up and running over to me, thrusting her hand out. "I'm Bella!"

"Bella, this is my friend Lucy. Lucy, this is my daughter, Bella," John says, still smiling. "But I guess you don't need me to introduce you!"

"Wanna see my dolls?" Bella asks, returning to her seat on the carpet. "Look! This one is Jasmine. She's a princess," she says matter-of-factly.

"Oh, she's beautiful!" I say, bending over to meet Bella at eye level.

"She's my most favorite, but you can play with her, too. I'm very good at sharing," Bella says, looking over at her father. "I'm a good sharer, right, Daddy?"

"That's right, sweetie. And sharing is very important," John answers seriously. "It's nice, and it makes your friends feel happy."

Is that what John was doing with all that money he gave me, I want to ask – *sharing?*

But obviously, I'm not going to bring it up in front of his daughter. It doesn't feel right.

"You can be Jasmine, and I'll be Ariel," says Bella happily, patting the floor on the ground next to her with her little hand, inviting me to sit down.

"Bella, Lucy is very busy with important work, and just came by to talk to Daddy for a minute," John explains patiently from his desk. "I don't think she wants to play with you right now. But I'll take a break soon and we can go to the park, how does that sound?"

"And do the swings?!" Bells asks excitedly, then turns to me. "Daddy is the best pusher! He lets me go way, way, way, all the way high up! But don't tell Mommy," she adds in a solemn whisper. "She's not a very good pusher. She doesn't go very high, and Daddy says it will hurt Mommy's feelings if I say Daddy's a better pusher."

I struggle to hold back a laugh as John exaggeratedly covers his face in mock embarrassment. But in the back of my mind I wonder, *who is Mommy?*

"Well, Lucy, what can I do for you?" John asks, "Before Bella can spill all of my secrets."

I smile at him, despite myself. My resolve to confront him is melting away, not that I would do it in front of his adorable little girl anyway.

"Uh, n...nothing..." I stammer. "Just... wanted to say thanks again for coffee yesterday."

"Don't mention it," John says, his smile growing even wider. I notice he has great teeth, perfectly straight and white. He must have worn his retainer every night since high school.

"Now can you play with me, Lucy?" Bella looks up at me with those big blue eyes and my heart melts a little. John tries to protest again when I notice another doll on the floor.

"Hey, is that a Madeline doll?" I ask eagerly.

"Madeline! Madeline! Madeline!" sings Bella, grabbing the doll and handing it to me.

"I had one just like this when I was a little girl," I say softly, looking over the cloth doll in her signature blue coat and yellow hat. "I wonder if they still..."

Without thinking, I sit down cross-legged on the ground next to Bella, dropping my purse at my side. I lift up the doll's coat to reveal a little scar on her stomach above her bloomers, stitched with red thread.

"Look!" I say happily, pointing out the scar to Bella. "They still put the scar on her! Do you know what that's from?"

"Oooo, let me see!" exclaims Bella, grabbing the doll from me to look at the red lines.

"Have you read any of the Madeline books?" I ask her.

"I can't read all the way yet. I know some words, but not books all the way. Daddy helps me. And I can spell my name!" she says proudly.

"That's very good! You must be really smart."

"Really smart," Bella repeats, to confirm it.

"Does your Daddy help you read the Madeline books?"

"Yes, I have some right here!" Bella answers, pulling a Madeline book out from underneath a coloring book.

"Have you read the one where Madeline gets her scar?"

"Hmmm..." Bella pulls an exaggerated thinking face, resting her chin on her fist and scrunching up her nose. Again, I force down a laugh. She is too darn cute.

"It's because she had appendicitis," I explain.

"What's pendis-tis?" Bella tries the word out in her mouth.

"Appendicitis," I explain, "Is like a tummy ache, but you have to go see the doctor to fix it. It's a good story."

"You help me read it?" Bella asks, clutching the doll and waving the book at me.

I look up at John, who I forgot was sitting there for a minute. He is gazing down at us with a softness in his eyes I've never seen before.

"Do you mind if I...?" I trail off. I don't want to cross any lines, but John seems unbothered.

"Please, not at all," he encourages. "You're doing me a favor."

With his permission, I start reading aloud from the book, keeping my voice low to try not to disturb John. At some point, Bella crawls off the floor into my lap and sticks her thumb in her mouth while I read to her.

When we finish the first book, I close it up and set it down. Bella reaches over and grabs another one at random from her pile and removes her thumb from her mouth to demand, "Another one!"

I look to John again and lift an eyebrow to ask for permission, assuming he'd prefer if I went to my desk and did some actual work.

"You heard the lady," John says, nodding his head. "That is, if you don't mind. I know you're busy."

"It's fine. I can catch up on it later." I grab the next book.

I lose count of how many books I read to Bella before I realize she's fallen asleep in my lap. John notices, too, and comes out from behind his desk to help gently lift her off of me. I watch silently as he tenderly places a little pillow underneath her blonde head and kisses her forehead while she sleeps.

"Thanks," he whispers to me. "I owe you one."

"She's adorable," I whisper back.

"I know," he says with a proud smile. "I'm so lucky."

I've never seen this side of John before, and it's honestly shocking. He's obviously a devoted father and is head over heels for this little girl.

It's really sweet, actually.

I exit his office, more confused than ever.

Maybe John really has changed, I think. Maybe he's the guy I thought I saw inside him all those years ago.

Is it possible he just gave me the money out of the goodness of his heart, rather than some ulterior motive?

Could he have changed that much?

10

JOHN

"No, Olivia, I can't. You know I have work today. Like every other weekday," I say into the phone, exasperated.

"Well, John, you'll just have to deal with it. I've been on a waiting list to see this doctor for months, and he finally has an opening today. I can't miss it," Olivia argues.

"What doctor?" I ask suspiciously. I would never begrudge Olivia changing our custody schedule to see a doctor for her health, of course. But knowing Olivia, it's probably a plastic surgeon, if she really has a doctor's appointment at all.

"He's a dermatologist," Olivia says defensively. "He's the best in town, and he has a waitlist about a mile long."

"A dermatologist? What do you need to see a dermatologist for?"

"Oh, just some maintenance things. A little touch up. Some Botox, maybe some fillers."

"Great, Olivia, just great. So you want me to take Bella on *your* custody day so you can go get a bunch of cosmetic procedures? How much does all that cost, anyway?"

"You didn't have any complaints about my so-called *cosmetic proce-dures* when we were dating," Olivia snaps, and I wince. "And for your information, I need to get my skin checked for cancer, too."

"You don't have skin cancer, Olivia," I say, picturing her flawless olive skin and rolling my eyes.

"You don't know that," she pouts. "I have a mole."

"Where?" I ask.

"That one on my shoulder. You know."

"Olivia, that's a freckle."

"Well, when you get your medical degree, I'll ask you," she retorts. "Anyway, I need to put this appointment on the credit card, and it's reaching the limit. Do you think you can pay that off soon?"

I inhale deeply and count to ten in my head so I don't explode with rage.

"Hello? John? Are you there?"

"Yeah, yeah, I'm here. You know there's no way I'll be able to get a sitter last-minute, right?"

"Duh, I couldn't get one either. That's why I called you. You are her father, after all."

"Right, and you're her mother, and you really need to stick to our custody schedule. You know I love having Bella, but I can't just bring her into work with me every time you feel like taking a day off from being a parent."

It's harsh, but true. This isn't the first time Olivia has asked – no, *demanded* – I take Bella for her on one of her scheduled days. I wouldn't mind if it was an emergency or if it only happened every once in a while, but it's becoming a regular occurrence.

"And why doesn't she have school again?" I ask, rubbing my palm against my forehead.

"Her class is going on a field trip to the zoo today. You know she doesn't like seeing the animals in cages," Olivia says.

"So she's missing more school," I sigh. "Fine, Olivia, but seriously, if this happens again, I'm going to contact a lawyer to have our custody agreement changed. I'm happy to have the time with Bella, but I need to be able to plan around it. Do you understand?"

"I call you for help with an emergency doctor visit and you threaten my custody of our daughter?" Olivia wails into the phone.

"Don't start with me, Olivia. I'll pick Bella up on my way in to work. Please, please have her dressed and ready to go. And you're welcome, by the way," I growl, angrily jabbing the phone to end the call.

I'm furious for the duration of the drive to Olivia's house, which used to be my home. But my anger dissipates as soon as I pull up and Bella flings open the front door and comes running toward the car.

Olivia follows behind her, carrying Bella's little pink backpack full of snacks, toys, and other ways to keep her entertained throughout the day.

Olivia looks beautiful, as usual, although with the feelings I have for her now I barely notice her appearance. She has perfectly even, tanned skin, offset by the white linen top she's wearing, paired with expensive jeans. Her dark, silky hair is pulled back in a high ponytail and she's wearing heels, accentuating her long, thin legs.

I hop out of the car to hug Bella and help strap her into her car seat, before Olivia kisses her goodbye. Olivia may have her faults as a person, and definitely as a partner, but she really does try to be a good mother to Bella. Sometimes, like today, I wish she'd try a little harder to co-parent with me.

"I'll drop her off before dinner," I tell Olivia tersely, not looking her in the eye.

"Oh, perfect," Olivia coos, placing one perfectly manicured hand on my arm. "Why don't you join us for dinner, then? I'll make something delicious."

The way Olivia swings between malicious and flirtatious never ceases to confound me.

"Not tonight, Olivia," I say, not wanting to start another argument, while thinking, *probably not ever.*

I'd love to have a better relationship with Olivia, for Bella's sake. But it's hard when the reason we broke up is because of her repetitive cheating, lying, and manipulating, and from what I can see, she hasn't changed since we were together.

Olivia and I met in college, and I was head over heels for her. She was the most stunning woman I'd ever seen, but she was also charming, funny, and wild. She made me feel things I'd never felt before. As cheesy as it may sound, she made me feel *alive*.

Being with Olivia was an adventure. She always had crazy ideas that compose some of my best memories, like the time in college she blindfolded me to drive me out to the middle of a field at night so we could watch a meteor shower and make love under the stars.

Her passionate nature had a dark side, too. We were always fighting, and I never knew what would set her off. She was moody, impatient, and selfish. But I had my own faults, too, and I figured nobody was perfect. And I thought Olivia was perfect, at least, for me. I thought she was *the one*, and that we would be together forever. We talked all the time about getting married and what our future would be like.

Then, after we graduated, I discovered Olivia cheated on me. Things hadn't been going well between us, and one night I overheard her talking on the phone. Her tone of voice alerted me that something was off.

I hate to admit it, but I found the proof going through her phone while she took a bath later that evening. She had a passcode, but I knew it was the same as my own: her birthday.

There were tons of text messages that made it clear that Olivia had been unfaithful – multiple times, with multiple guys. I felt sick to my stomach when I read through everything. I couldn't even confront her that night, I just left her unlocked phone out to discover when she came out of the bathroom and went to sleep at a buddy's house.

When we talked about it the next day, Olivia was tearful and apologetic. I was going to break up with her, but she convinced me that she would change. She said it was all just a stupid mistake and that she didn't want me to throw away our future together over this.

So I gave her another chance. And another chance after that. And every time, she cheated on me again. She broke my heart.

In our arguments, she'd even accuse me of cheating, too, which I never did. At least, not on her. I never cheated on Olivia, not once. Even when she suggested it as a way to "even the score."

The final straw was the last time I caught her cheating. I hadn't even been looking for it, but she'd left her email account open on the computer we shared and seeing my name in an email preview caught my eye. I clicked through several of the emails and was disgusted to see how she talked about me to the guy she was seeing. She said she didn't love me, she only wanted to be with me for my money, and she was afraid to leave me.

There was no coming back from that. I broke it off for good.

I'll admit that I had moments of weakness, times when Olivia would call me up in the night. If I'd been out drinking with friends, my inhibitions lowered, I would let her come over and we'd have wild, crazy sex like we did at the beginning of our relationship.

One of those times, Olivia got pregnant.

Whether it was truly an accident or not, I'll never know, although I have my suspicions.

Olivia wanted to get back together, like she always did. She said that a baby would bring us together and that things would be different. Olivia wanted us to get married like we'd always planned and raise the child together.

At this point, Olivia was still living in the house that we shared (and I paid for), while I'd moved into my own bachelor pad. Olivia was only supposed to stay in the house until she found her own place, and then I could sell it. Once she became pregnant, I told her that she should just keep the house, if she wanted it. There was plenty of room for a baby there, and she wouldn't have to worry about looking for a new home or the hassle of moving while she was pregnant and becoming a new mom.

But I didn't want to be with her anymore. The trust between us was so irreparably shattered, I couldn't look at her or love her the same way, not even with a baby in the picture.

So we stayed separated, although I tried to help as much as possible during her pregnancy. I went to the house nearly every day to stock the fridge with healthy food, help Olivia build the nursery, and take care of her when she was nauseous. I went to every doctor's appointment and every ultrasound.

All the while, I was never one hundred percent convinced that

Olivia was carrying my child. Can you blame me? Even if Olivia was being honest, which she didn't have the best track record for, I didn't know if she could even be sure who the baby's father was.

But when Bella was born and I saw her blue eyes, the exact same shape and color as mine, I both fell in love and knew with absolute certainty that she was mine.

Olivia and I came up with a shared custody agreement we could both live with. I continued to pay the mortgage on what was now just Olivia's house, and we agreed on child support payments. We also agreed that Olivia, who hadn't worked a job since college, would be a stay-at-home mom. By that time, I was working long nights making Room Publishing into a juggernaut, and we both thought it was best if Olivia could devote herself full-time to taking care of Bella.

But now that Bella is in preschool, and soon to be full-time at an elementary school, I don't think it's the worst idea for Olivia to get a job. Not that she needs the money – I make sure she has everything she could ever want. She's the mother of my child, I have the means, and I want to keep her happy. I consider myself extremely fortunate to be able to take care of my child and her mother financially. But Olivia definitely takes advantage of that, and today's "emergency visit" to get Botox, which I'm sure I'll be paying for, is just another example.

I think Olivia is lonely – she may be a lot of things, but she's not the type of single mother who brings a different guy around every week. I'm sure she dates, or whatever, but she's very conscientious about only doing so when I have Bella. To my knowledge, she hasn't gotten serious enough with any guy to want to introduce him to Bella.

Maybe having a job, even just some sort of freelance or part-time job, would help her feel better. At the very least, it might keep her preoccupied from trying to convince me to take her back.

Because in spite of everything, Olivia still thinks we should be together. Ideally, I'd love to make it work with her and be able to live together with Bella as a happy family. But I'm too hurt over what Olivia has done, and she's still the same person who did all those terrible things when we were together.

I've made that very clear to her, but it doesn't stop her from constantly trying to tempt me with invitations to have a glass of wine when I drop off Bella, or to stay for a "sleepover" on nights I've helped put Bella to bed at her house. I never give in, though. Not even when I look at her and think I can still see the captivating, wild girl she was in college, dragging me along on her crazy adventures.

I miss those days, and I miss how we used to be, but I can't go back.

I'm thinking about all this as I blast Disney songs for Bella to warble along from her car seat. I chime in occasionally, making Bella giggle hysterically when I purposely mess up the words, belting "a whole new squirrel" instead of "a whole new world."

Olivia's "emergencies" have become common enough that no one in the office blinks twice at me bringing Bella in. We even have a little routine of sorts. She'll play with her toys in my office while I work until about midmorning, then we go together to the nearby coffee shop for hot chocolate and coffee. Then I work a bit more before taking a long lunch break and walking Bella to the park. After a few more hours of work, during which Bella usually naps, I either bring her home with or take her back to her mother's house.

This morning, as soon as Bella and I settle into my office, I look at my calendar and realize Olivia couldn't have picked a worse day to pull this stunt. I have an insane amount of work to finish, and I'll probably have to return to the office to get it all done after I take Bella home for dinner. I sigh, resigning myself to what will probably be a 14-hour day, when Lucy comes rushing in.

I glance up at her as she opens my office door. She looks flustered, her pale cheeks flushed pink and her brow furrowed. Is she angry?

She opens her mouth to speak, but before she says anything, she notices Bella playing on the floor.

"Lucy!" I say with a smile, because I can't help it. Even though she looks upset, I'm happy to see her.

"Lucy!" repeats Bella. She's in that phase of mimicking everything, which can be both adorable and alarming. She stands up to greet Lucy, reaching out one small hand. "I'm Bella!"

"Bella, this is my friend Lucy. Lucy, this is my daughter, Bella," I say unnecessarily. "But I guess you don't need me to introduce you!"

"Wanna see my dolls?" Bella asks, sitting back down and eagerly showing off her toys. "Look! This one is Jasmine. She's a princess."

I wonder what Lucy is thinking. I see her expression shift from anger to confusion, and then she is quickly charmed by Bella.

"Oh, she's beautiful!" Lucy says, crouching down to the same height as Bella.

"She's my most favorite, but you can play with her, too. I'm very good at sharing," Bella says, glancing at me. "I'm a good sharer, right, Daddy?"

"That's right, sweetie. And sharing is very important," I tell her. Bella's class at preschool has been working on sharing, and Bella takes it very seriously. "It's nice, and it makes your friends feel happy."

"You can be Jasmine, and I'll be Ariel," Bella instructs Lucy.

"Bella, Lucy is very busy with important work, and just came by to talk to Daddy for a minute," I explain, assuming Lucy would prefer to get back to work. "I don't think she wants to play with you right now. But I'll take a break soon and we can go to the park, how does that sound?"

"And do the swings?!" Bella asks, then faces Lucy and says, "Daddy is the best pusher! He lets me go way, way, way, all the way high up! But don't tell Mommy," she whispers. "She's not a very good pusher. She doesn't go very high, and Daddy says it will hurt Mommy's feelings if I say Daddy's a better pusher."

At this, I slap my hands against my face, covering my eyes in mock embarrassment while Bella giggles. I should let Lucy escape before Bella can say anything that might truly be mortifying.

"Well, Lucy, what can I do for you?" I ask. "Before Bella can spill all of my secrets."

Lucy smiles and appears to carefully considering her words.

"Uh, nothing... Just... wanted to say thanks again for coffee yesterday."

It's a lie, I can tell. Her stammer and blush give her away. She's a terrible liar. What did she really want to talk about?

"Don't mention it." I smile back.

"Now can you play with me Lucy?" Bella pleads. I try to tell Bella that Lucy wants to get back to work, but then I see Lucy's face light up.

"Hey, is that a Madeline doll?" Lucy exclaims.

"Madeline! Madeline! Madeline!" sings Bella.

"I had one just like this when I was a little girl."

Before I know it, Bella has clambered into Lucy's lap while Lucy reads to her softly. Lucy glances over at me occasionally, tacitly seeking my permission to stay and read to Bella. I don't mind at all – not only does it give me the chance to get some work done, but I enjoy having Lucy nearby.

With Lucy's reading voice as a soothing background noise, I fly through my work. When I look up, I notice Bella has fallen asleep in Lucy's lap.

I come out from behind my desk and gently lift Bella off of Lucy, transferring her to a blanket spread out on the floor. I tuck a small pillow from her backpack under her mess of curls, brushing a few locks back to kiss her forehead while she sleeps.

"Thanks," I whisper to Lucy. "I owe you one."

"She's adorable."

"I know," I say, beaming. "I'm so lucky."

Lucy quietly leaves the office, and I realize that I miss the sound of her voice, her presence.

What has gotten into me?

Seeing how kind and patient Lucy is with my daughter reminds me of what a good person she is, and always has been. Back in high school, when I was still acting like a jerk because I thought it was "cool," she was the one who really made me want to be different.

I remember how excited I was when we finally kissed, after months of longing on my part. I hate how sad she looked when she pulled away. She told me later that we couldn't be together because of the way I had treated her in the past.

I was devastated, but I couldn't really blame her, even more so looking back at it now. I was awful to her, a bully. She was the new kid, and kind of a prude, and I was the popular football jock. I'm embarrassed when I think about how I behaved, how I must have made her start at a new school so much harder than it already was.

Reflecting on it now, I almost can't believe she agreed to work for me, even if she did really need the job. If the tables were turned, I don't know if I would be able to set aside my pride. But that's just the kind of person Lucy is.

I think about the money I sent her and feel ashamed that I thought it could even make a dent in the debt I owe Lucy, unbeknownst to her.

Once again, Lucy Myers is a living, breathing reminder for me to do better. To *be* better.

And I'm glad to have her here.

It's not just that, though. Lucy is a good person, but she's also gorgeous, honest, hardworking, direct, and funny. We have a lot of common interests, not to mention our similar backgrounds. If I met Lucy out at a bar, even without having ever known her, she's exactly the type of person I would be attracted to.

Maybe in another lifetime. For now, I'll have to settle for enjoying her company as an employee and trying to make amends for how horrible I was to her when we were younger. If I'm lucky, maybe I can prove to her that I'm a different person, someone worthy of her trust, of her friendship.

As I'm musing, Bella stirs from her nest on the floor.

"Can we go to the park now, Daddy?" she asks, her voice groggy with sleep. I push my high school memories and thoughts of Lucy out of my mind, for now. I need to focus on taking care of my daughter.

"Of course we can, baby. Want to get a hot chocolate on the way?"

11

LUCY

I've been working at Room Publishing for over a week now, and I feel more comfortable and settled in than I expected to. I'm even familiar with having John as a boss. As a matter of fact, it's kind of nice seeing him around the office.

He's kind, generous, and patient. I've seen how he treats the rest of his staff and how he treats me. He really seems different from when we were kids. Watching him interact with his daughter was the final piece of the puzzle for me – John McQueen has changed, and definitely for the better.

On Friday, I'm taking a break for lunch when my cell phone buzzes with a text. It's from John – we've never texted before, but I programmed his number, along with Greta and everyone else in my department, into my phone when I started working at Room. You never know when you'll need to contact someone from work.

Hey Lucy, this is John McQueen. Was wondering if you wanted to join the team for a happy hour after work this evening?

. . .

My heart skips a beat at the message. He's asking me out for happy hour? That means drinks, right? But we wouldn't be alone... he says the whole team will be there. So that's not inappropriate, right?

What would it be like though, I wonder, to have drinks alone with John? To go out on an actual date with him? I picture his tall, athletic frame, his broad shoulders and blonde hair, those deep blue eyes... I know he's only a few yards away from me in his office, but I'm still looking forward to the next time I can see him.

What is the matter with me?

Over the last few days, I've felt old feelings for John bubbling under the surface. Instead of anger or annoyance, I feel almost giddy when I see him. He has the same good looks and charm he's always had, but now he's humble and thoughtful, as well.

He's come a long way since those days of dumping soda on me in the cafeteria.

But he's still my boss, and I'm uncomfortable having these feelings for someone I work for. I have to play it safe.

Hi John, thanks for the invite, but I have a lot of work to do still and will probably have to stay late. :(

I don't actually have a lot of work to do, and was planning on going home and getting drunk alone in front of the TV after work, but I feel like it's best if I just say no.

As if he can sense my reluctance, John texts back:

Everyone will be there and it's a great way to bond with the rest of the office. We do it at least once a month, so if you can't make this one, you should come to the next! If you change your mind, feel free to stop by later.

· · ·

He adds the name and address of the bar where everyone is meeting later, and before I can stop myself, I text back:

Okay, I'll try to come for at least a little bit tonight!

The rest of the day drags by as I look forward to the happy hour after work with everyone, especially John. I'm excited to see what he's like with the team outside of work, particularly after a few drinks.

I scan my outfit and wish I'd worn something cuter to work today than a plain black sleeveless dress, leggings, and a red cardigan. Thankfully, I brought heels to wear to work today, even though I walked to the office in flats and was planning on changing back into them.

As the workday comes to an end, everyone is chatting eagerly about happy hour. It feels good when some of my colleagues – besides John – invite me along. It's nice to fit in.

I intentionally wait until almost everyone has already left the office to give credibility to my story about needing to work late. Then I head to the restroom, where I carefully touch up my makeup and add a coat of the red lipstick. I remove the leggings from underneath the dress, thankful I shaved my legs this morning. After I pull off the cardigan, I peer at myself in the mirror.

Does my short black dress look too sexy on its own? I put the cardigan back on, then take it off again. *Why the hell not?* I pull my hair out of its low ponytail and let it fall in loose waves around my shoulders, combing through it lightly with my fingers. Along with the heels I decided to keep on, I look pretty good.

I stroll out of the building, flinging my purse over my shoulder as I walk to the bar that John mentioned. Fortunately it's not far from the office, and I can walk the distance, even in heels.

When I enter the bar, a whimsical little hole-in-the-wall decorated with strings of lights and paper lanterns, I immediately spot a bunch of people from work crowded around a large table in the back.

I make my way over to them, feeling nervous. I'm self-conscious, and overly aware of my bare arms and legs. *Why did I take my cardigan off?* Now I'm wishing I'd brought it with me instead of leaving it flung over the back of my chair at the office.

As I approach, one of the other girls from the office lets out a low whistle, while one of the guys feigns a catcall.

"Ow, ow, Lucy!" Jacob shouts with a grin. He's a fellow editor, and I'm pretty sure he's gay. He's super nice, and we've had lunch together a couple of times since I started working at Room. "Looking good!"

"Wow, Lucy, you sure clean up nice!" Martha comments. She's around my age, also from my department. She pulls out the chair next to her, offering me the seat. I notice, with both pleasure and anxiety, that it's directly across the table from John, who is eyeing me strangely.

"Okay, okay. You guys, calm down," John teases. "Just because we're not at work doesn't mean you can harass each other."

"Sure, boss," Jacob says, grinning and throwing back a tequila shot.

I'm embarrassed by all the attention, and for a moment I wish I hadn't made the effort with my appearance. But then I catch John furtively checking me out as I sit, and decide it was worth it.

A margarita and a shot appear in front of me, and a platter of chips and salsa is passed around. Everyone is working on a buzz, and the volume of our table increases with every round.

I wasn't planning to stay long, but I'm having such a good time chatting with everyone. John was right, it is a great way to connect with the team. Everyone at work has been friendly so far, and after tonight, it seems like they'll feel more like friends than coworkers.

Martha and I click, discovering that we go to the same gym and promising to go together soon. I happily consider introducing her to Jen, knowing they will get along.

Jacob invites me to go to brunch sometime with him and his boyfriend, confirming my suspicions.

"And you should bring a date, of course! I'm assuming you have a man?" Jacob wiggles his eyebrows at me suggestively.

Before I can help myself, my eyes slide over to John, who has broken away from the conversation on his side of the table and is now listening attentively for my answer.

"No, no man. No boyfriend, nothing like that," I confess.

"Be still, my heart!" Jacob says with exaggerated shock. "A stunner like you? Do you have any prospects?" Jacob leans forward in his chair and props his elbow up on the table, perching his chin on his fist.

"Not a one," I answer happily, noticing that John raises an eyebrow at my response.

"Well, we'll have to change that, won't we?" Jacob pulls out his cell phone. "I have a ton of friends I'd love to set you up with."

"Jake, leave the poor woman alone," John says. He's joking, but there's a serious edge to his voice.

"Yeah, Jake," Martha chimes in. "Who says she wants a boyfriend? Maybe she wants to be single. Or maybe she wants a girlfriend!"

"Are you offering?" I turn to Martha, grinning.

"I'm taken, but I've got some friends..." Martha says.

"No, no, only kidding." I'm ready to turn the conversation away from my love life, or rather, the lack thereof. Feeling emboldened by the tequila in my system, I brazenly turn to John and ask, "Aren't you single, too, John?"

"Oh, John's single alright," Jacob answers before John can open his mouth. "He doesn't date."

"How do you know?" John asks suspiciously.

"You've never brought anyone to happy hour, and the only woman who has ever visited you at the office is your baby mama," Jacob confirms.

"Very astute, Jacob." John rolls his eyes. "If you ever decide to quit working at Room, you'd make a great detective."

"So I'm right," Jacob crows.

"Yeah, sure, I'm single," John admits. Is it my imagination, or do his eyes flicker over to me as he says it?

Someone else changes the subject, and we all talk and laugh

through several more rounds. People are slowly exiting, the table becoming emptier until somehow, it's just John and I left.

I glance at John across the table, nervousness and excitement running through me. I've had so much to drink that he's blurry, as if I've already taken my contacts out.

"Well, um..." I say uncomfortably, all of my bravado gone now that there's no one else around. "I guess I should get going..."

"No, wait." John gestures for me to stay seated. "I was hoping to get a chance to talk to you alone."

"Really?" My heart leaps up to my throat.

"Yeah, I wanted to check in with you. To ask you how it's going at the office. Is everyone showing you the ropes and helping you out?"

I feel a little deflated at his line of questioning but assure him that everything at Room has been lovely so far. I start to leave again, but this time John lightly grabs my arm to stop me.

"Actually..." he says, clearing his throat and starting over. "Actually, I wanted to talk to you about something else, too."

"Yeah?" I ask, barely able to breathe.

"Do you remember back in high school," he begins, and I can hear a slight slur in his voice that gives away how much he's had to drink. "The last time we saw each other?"

I can't believe he's bringing this up. Of course I remember. Now that we work together and John is back in my life, I think about it all the time. Still, I'm so surprised he's bringing it up, I can't find the words to respond.

"It's stupid, of course you don't remember," John mumbles, almost to himself. "That was so long ago, and I probably didn't mean much of anything to you..."

That's where he's wrong, but I let him continue rather than correcting him. He looks me directly in the eye, and his piercing eye contact sobers me up instantly.

"Maybe you don't remember everything... how awful I was to you back then. But I want you to know that I really took it to heart, what you said. About us not being able to be together," he clarified. "Because of how I treated you."

I remember that moment perfectly. I remember how hard it was to stay away from him after that, when all I wanted was to spend the summer wrapped in his arms. I think about the time he kissed me, and it's almost like I can still feel his lips on mine.

As I glance at him now, his eyes have gone hazy, and I think maybe he's remembering that moment, too.

"Anyway, I just wanted to say again that I'm really, truly sorry," John adds humbly. "At the time, I knew the way I had acted towards you wasn't okay. But I think when you turned me down, I was more wrapped up in feeling sorry for myself than anything. Anyway, looking back, I now fully understand how wrong I was, and want to give you the apology I still feel I owe you. And I also want to thank you."

"For what?" I ask in surprise, finally regaining my voice.

"I've given a lot of thought over the years to what you said, and it changed how I treated people after that. You were right, and if you hadn't called me out, who knows how long it would've taken me to learn that lesson. I'm just sorry I had to learn it at your expense."

"Well, it's water under the bridge now," I say, still unable to believe we are having this conversation. Since things are already so surreal, and because I'm still tipsy, I boldly add, "Is that why you gave me all that money?"

John looks at me sharply. "You mean the sign-on bonus?"

"Yeah. Except it wasn't really a sign-on bonus, was it?"

"How did you know?" John asks.

"I have my ways," I reply mysteriously, mentally thanking Jen for her brilliant detective work.

"Well, I'll admit, I still felt like I owed you," John sighs. "And it was the perfect opportunity to help you out without you knowing. Honestly, I probably should've been giving all new hires a sign-on bonus, and I will from now on."

"That much of one?" I ask, raising one eyebrow skeptically. Except, because of the tequila, both eyebrows shoot up and one eye closes in an awkward wink.

"Probably not," John laughs. "But I plan to build some sort of bonus into their contracts, at least."

"I'd like to pay you back," I insist, even though I know that I have no way of doing so at the moment. "Maybe we could take a little bit out of my next few paychecks or something?"

"Absolutely not," John says firmly. "Please, consider it a favor you're doing me. Although I can never really repay you, both for how I acted back then and for how you helped me, it does a lot to ease my guilt."

"Well, I'd hate for you to lose sleep over me," I joke, then realize how it sounds. I blush, searching John's face for a reaction. He looks stunned, then like he's making a decision about something.

"Right," John says dryly. "Hey, do you want to get another drink? Or, better yet, want to come back to my place for a nightcap?"

"Oh!" I say in surprise. John is inviting me to his place? Is he saying what I think he's saying?

Is he asking as my boss? Or an old friend I went to high school with?

Or something else?

"Come on, it'll be fun!" John's teasing grin returns. "I think I even have my old yearbook buried somewhere."

"You want me to sign your yearbook?" I tease back, unable to resist.

"H.A.K.A.S.!" John spells out, chuckling. "Isn't that what everyone always wrote? What does that even mean again?"

"Have a kick ass summer," I reply, laughing along with him. "Or L.Y.L.A.S."

"What's that one?"

"Love you like a sister," I crow.

"Yikes, I don't think I got any of those in mine." John cringes exaggeratedly. "But we should probably go check. What do you say?"

I pretend to weigh my options, even though I already know what my answer will be. In fact, I think a part of me knew something like this was coming all along, from the moment I first saw John McQueen's name pop up in my email inbox.

"I say... Yes."

12

———

JOHN

I can't believe I just asked Lucy to come back to my apartment. What was I thinking?

Okay, I know exactly what I was thinking. What I'm still thinking, as I gaze at her in her sexy black dress, with her full lips painted red and her hair falling softly around her face. Her cheeks are flushed with alcohol and she has a loose, relaxed grin on her face. I don't know that I've ever seen her look so carefree, not even when we were kids.

It's insanely sexy, and she's driving me crazy.

To my shock, she agrees. But maybe it's not so surprising after all. I could just be imagining it, but I feel like there's something between us.

I have to be careful, though – I am, after all, her boss. I don't want to put her in an uncomfortable situation or pressure her in any way. Not only because it would be an HR nightmare, but because I genuinely care about her. I know, as her boss, that I'm in a position of power over her and I don't want to abuse that, especially when there is alcohol involved.

Maybe she's just coming over as an old friend. Perhaps she really just wants to reminisce and look at old yearbook photos, like I suggested.

I'd be lucky to have her even as a friend, all things considered.

I resolve to tread lightly and not make the first move, if it even comes to that. Which it won't.

"Let me just settle up at the bar," I tell Lucy.

"I'll come with you." She grabs her bag and rises to her feet. It gives me another chance to look at her body in that tight dress again. At work, she usually dresses like a librarian, hiding her body under boxy blazers and flowy skirts. But now, I can see how lithe and fit she is. I want to grab her by the waist, run my fingers through her long hair, bite that pouty lower lip... but I shake my head to force the images out of my brain.

Not going to happen, I tell myself sternly.

We cross the few steps to the bar, and I notice a few heads turning our way. I can't tell if they are looking at me, Lucy, or both.

"Here you go, McQueen." The friendly bartender passes me the bill. He's usually here when the team comes in for happy hour, and I've come in alone a few times to grab a beer and watch a game. We've gotten to know each other a bit, and he's under strict instructions not to let any of my staff pay for their drinks when we're here and to save the tab for me.

"Thanks, Joey," I say, sliding over my credit card without even looking at the receipt. I try to do it smoothly, but Lucy must have seen the bill anyway.

"You paid for everyone?" she asks, eyes wide.

"Yeah," I reply casually, not wanting to make a big deal out of it. "I always do. I figure it's the least I can do to show my appreciation, you know?"

"And how often do you do this?"

"It depends on how often a lot of us can get together, sometimes it's weekly, sometimes it's once a month. It's fun though, right?"

"Yeah. Well, thank you. That's really generous of you."

"It's no big deal," I say, and to me, it really isn't. I try to pay my staff fairly, but I know how much they all make, and there's definitely a great disparity between my income and theirs. It's only fair that I pick up the bill, especially since it's technically a work gathering, even though we've all become friends.

After closing the tab, Lucy and I walk out the door. I feel a strong urge to grab her hand and hold it in mine as we walk, but I restrain myself.

It's a nice night, and we've both had a lot to drink, so I suggest we walk back to my place. It's not far, and some days I walk to work instead of driving. With Chicago weather, though, you can't walk everywhere year-round, and I hate taking public transportation. And with Bella, I never know when I'll need to drive to her mother's house, even on workdays, so it's best if I have the car handy. Right now, my car is parked in the garage at the office, where it will be safe overnight.

As we walk, we continue to exchange crazy stories about our high school days. I'm having such a good time that we're in front of my building before I know it.

"Oh, my God, this is where you live?" Lucy exclaims as we approach the front steps of the building.

"Yeah, why?"

Lucy laughs. "I live just a couple of blocks from here. You can almost see my building!" She peers off into the distance looking for it. The doorman lets us in, and once we're in the elevator, Lucy adds, "We don't have a doorman, though. Your place is definitely nicer."

"We?" I ask, raising an eyebrow.

"Oh, Jen and I live in the same building," Lucy explains. "We both have our own apartments, but we spend so much time together we're practically roommates."

"That's nice," I smile, thinking of my college days in the dorms. "So you two have stayed friends this whole time?"

"Yeah, she's the best," Lucy gushes, then begins to sing Jennifer's praises. She stops mid-sentence, though, when I unlock the door to my apartment and we step inside.

"Wow," she breathes, after gazing around in silence. "John, this place is amazing!"

I don't spend a lot of time at home unless I'm sleeping, and I barely notice my surroundings anymore. I picked this place solely on its proximity to the office. I know it's a nice apartment, but now I try to look at it through Lucy's eyes.

It's very much a bachelor pad, with black leather couches, a large flat screen TV, and sleek, modern kitchen that only gets used to warm up leftover takeout. The decor is modern and minimal, with stark white walls that are sparsely covered with framed art pieces that came with the apartment.

"Thanks," I say, shrugging. "Why don't you have a seat, and I'll grab us that nightcap."

"Wait, is your daughter here?" Lucy asks, lowering her voice as if we might wake Bella.

"She's with her mother this weekend."

The open floor plan allows Lucy to watch me from the couch while I rummage in the kitchen for glasses. Having her eyes on me makes me nervous, even though it shouldn't. She's just a coworker, maybe a friend, I tell myself. *Get it together.*

"What do you think?" I ask. "Should we switch to wine? Or keep drinking tequila?"

"Hmm. Do you have any margarita mixer?"

"I can do even better than that." I pull a large glass bottle off of the bar cart in the kitchen. I methodically pour clear liquor into a cocktail shaker, then add ice from the freezer and shake it. I strain the chilled liquid into two glasses, then top each one off with a squeeze of fresh lime juice from the fridge.

"Is that a shot?" Lucy looks confused.

"Have you ever had Casa Dragones?" I ask, handing her the glass. "It's a sipping tequila. I had it for the first time on vacation in Mexico a few years back, and now it's my favorite liquor."

"You don't have to mix it with anything?" Lucy eyes the drink suspiciously.

"You can, but it's best as is. Try it," I encourage her.

"Okay." Lucy raises the glass to her lips. "Oh, wait!" She stops suddenly, before she's had a sip.

"What?"

"Cheers," she says, clinking her glass against mine as I stand above her. "To..."

"To your first happy hour with the Room crew," I finish, smiling and taking a drink. "May there be many more to come."

I start to sit down, then remember what we came here for. "Let me see if I can find that yearbook!"

I set my drink on the glass coffee table and run to my bedroom. It's mostly clean, I notice gratefully, still sweeping some random debris off my bedside table into a drawer. Because what if Lucy comes in here at some point?

Not that there would be any reason for her to do so.

I step over to my bookshelf and find the dusty book at the very bottom. I'm surprised I've kept the yearbook for this long, and that it has survived the moves to college, the old house, and to this apartment. I guess I always thought there would come a time when I would want to look at it again.

"Found it!" I call out triumphantly, hurrying back to the living room where Lucy is sipping her drink. "How do you like it?" I ask, nodding at her glass.

"It's delicious," Lucy replies happily, and I can see that she has kicked off her heels and tucked her feet underneath herself on the couch. "I've never had anything like it."

"I told you, it's the best! The problem is, now you're not going to want any other tequila ever again," I joke.

"You've spoiled me!" Lucy groans. "How will I ever drink plebeian, rail tequila again?"

"Maybe that's my trap to get you to come over again, so you can have the good stuff," I tease, grinning.

"Or maybe I'll just have to switch to vodka," Lucy fires back without missing a beat, and I laugh.

I sit next to her on the couch, trying to keep a respectful distance while still being able to peruse the yearbook together. "Let's find our pictures, shall we?"

"Oh, no," Lucy groans. "Has anyone ever taken a *good* yearbook photo?"

I flip through the pages, and because I was a senior and a year ahead of Lucy, my picture comes up first. And there I am, in a little square photo wedged between Casey MacMillan and Anthony Menard. I'm in my football uniform, since athletes wear their jersey on picture day. My hair is in an outdated style, and my smile doesn't reach my eyes.

"You look pretty much the same," Lucy observes. "You just wear suits now instead of a jersey."

"Yeah," I say, looking at the forced smile in the photo and thinking about how much happier I am now. Back then, I was under my dad's thumb, forced to play a sport I didn't really care about, and not being true to myself. I think about how far I've come from that angry, confused teenager and feel a wave of gratitude. "Now let's see yours."

I flip a few pages until I find Lucy. Her pretty little face peers back at me. She was always beautiful, but this photo must have been taken before she had her makeover. Her dirty blonde hair, now a lighter shade, is pulled back in a tight ponytail. Her uniform blouse is buttoned all the way up, even though most girls like to only button it as far as they could without getting in trouble. She's smiling so hard that she's almost squinting.

"I look terrible," Lucy moans, trying to cover the photo with her hand.

"No, it's cute," I protest, trying to brush her hand away.

We pretend to fight over the yearbook, both of us reaching for it at the same time. Our knees and thighs are now pressed together, and I manage to grab the book and hold it out of Lucy's reach. She lunges for it, falling on top of me on the couch, laughing breathlessly. I'm nearly flat on my back and she's above me, smiling down into my face.

We lock eyes, and it takes everything in me not to pull her down for a kiss.

But I don't have to, because before I know it, she's closed the distance between our faces. She kisses me.

I drop the book on the floor and run my hands through Lucy's hair, just like I've been dreaming. I grab her hips, pulling her closer so that she's straddling me on the couch, her dress hiked up almost to her waist.

We're kissing passionately, like a couple of horny teenagers. My hands are all over Lucy's body, and she starts to unbutton my shirt. I can't believe this is happening. I can barely think at all, but my promise to myself from earlier jumps to the front of my mind.

"Wait, wait," I pant, grabbing Lucy firmly by the shoulders and pulling her lips off of mine for a moment.

"What's wrong?" Her lips are swollen from kissing, her hair is tousled and wild, and her dress is sliding down her shoulders. I want nothing more than to ravish her, but I know I have to be responsible.

"Are you sure you want to do this?" I ask quietly.

"If we don't, I might explode," Lucy laughs. Then, seeing how serious I am, she solemnly responds, "Yes, I'm sure, John."

"Because you're technically my employee, and I don't want to make you do anything that you don't—"

Lucy interrupts my chivalry by pressing her mouth to mine again. I start to remove her dress when she pushes my arms down, stopping me.

"Wha- what is it?" I ask, desperately hoping she hasn't changed her mind already.

"Are you drunk?" she asks, peering into my eyes suspiciously. "Because I don't want to, I don't know, take advantage if you're..."

I laugh. "Lucy, I'm not drunk, I promise," I say truthfully. I might be tipsy, but not to the point that I feel out of control. "Wait, are you drunk?"

"A little," Lucy admits playfully. "But not so much that I'm doing anything I don't want to be doing."

"And what do you want to do?" I question huskily.

"I could tell you," Lucy says, leaning forward in my lap to whisper into my ear, "But I think I'd rather show you."

With that, I can't hold back anymore. I stand up off the couch, lifting Lucy with me. She wraps her legs around my waist, and I grip her rear to carry her off to my bedroom, mouths intertwined the entire way.

Once we're in my room, I set her gently on top of the covers, standing above her at the foot of the bed. I help her slowly slide her black dress over her head, and when she lays back, I stop for a moment to admire her.

Her long, golden hair is fanned out across my pillows. Her lipstick has smeared off, and her full lips are smiling up at me. Her fair skin is flawless, glowing in the soft light of the bedside lamp. She's wearing a simple matching set, a black cotton bra and underwear, and her body is incredible – petite, yet with a sexy hourglass shape. I can't believe Lucy Myers is here in my bed, half-naked and grinning at me expectantly.

"God, Lucy, you're so beautiful."

As I drop my pants and finish unbuttoning my shirt, I'm suddenly anxious. I've been with plenty of women, but this isn't just some girl I met out at a bar or a blind date. This is Lucy, the girl I've been dreaming about for years.

Still in my boxers, I kneel between her legs on the bed and start kissing my way up one silky thigh. When I reach her black panties, I stop and trail my tongue down the other leg. When I'm done, I lean forward and kiss my way up her taut stomach to her soft breasts, inhaling her light, floral scent when I reach her neck.

She's moaning softly beneath me, running her hands up and down my back and shoulders. I tug the cups of her bra down, revealing her pert, pink nipples. I caress and lick them as she cries out, arching her back against me.

Unable to resist, I move back down between her legs and slip off her little black panties. Lucy grips my shoulders, urging me on. I tease her, kissing lightly around her upper thighs before finally putting my mouth on her sex.

As I move my tongue in slow, tantalizing circles, Lucy purrs with delight.

"Oh, yes, John. That feels so good. Yes, please don't stop," she murmurs with her eyes screwed shut and her head thrown back.

For a split second, I picture Lucy's sad face after I kissed her in high school. It's a stark contrast to the look of unadulterated pleasure on her now as I lap at her relentlessly. I laugh a little to myself, and the vibrations of my voice bring Lucy closer to the edge.

"Wait, stop," she moans, tugging on my arms to pull me up above her. "I'm not ready yet."

She uses her toes to hook the waistband of my underwear, efficiently sliding them off.

"Nice." I grin down at her.

"Yeah, well," she says modestly, "I guess you could say I've learned a thing or two since high school."

Lucy reaches for me, wrapping her small, warm hand around my length and slowly starts to pump it. I sigh as she guides the tip to her slick opening, teasing me by rubbing my cock up and down against her most sensitive spot.

"Are you ready?" she whispers.

"Yes, please," I beg.

Then she slides her hand away and arches her back so that I'm finally, finally inside her.

"Oh, my God," I groan lustfully as we grind against each other, matching our pace.

"You feel so good, John," Lucy yelps, biting her lip and breathing heavily.

I grab her hands, pinning them with mine above her head while devouring her mouth.

"John... I'm going to..." Lucy cries, and I feel her body clenching around me, taking me to the point of no return.

Our bodies convulse, climaxing together. I close my eyes, practically seeing stars as my body jerks uncontrollably.

Afterward, she lays in my arms as I stroke her hair, both of us struggling to catch our breath. The moment is so perfect, I never want it to end. I don't know how long we stay like that, but when I ask if she wants a glass of water, I realize she's fallen asleep.

I consider getting up to brush my teeth, but she's still in my arms. I don't want to disturb her. She looks so beautiful with her lashes brushing her still-flushed cheeks.

"Good night, Lucy," I whisper, softly pressing my lips to her forehead before drifting off to sleep.

13

LUCY

I'm in that strange place between awake and unconsciousness when I realize I'm not in my own bed.

My eyes fling open, now wide awake, and I feel a warm body pressed against mine.

As I become more alert, I remember. It's John, and this is his bed, his apartment.

I rewind further to happy hour at the bar, to me and John being the only ones left, and then coming back here.

And then... what we did together, right here in this bed.

I smile in spite of myself, but I'm completely panicked.

I can see the moonlight streaming through the window, telling me it's not morning yet. I glance over at John's sleeping face and am unsurprised to see that he's still devastatingly handsome even when he's unconscious.

My body fills with anxiety and dread. How I'm going to face John after this? I don't know what to do, but I know I have to get out of here, so I can think clearly.

I slip out of bed, slowly and carefully, to avoid waking John. I'm afraid to even breathe too hard in case it alerts him to my movement. I grab my dress and underwear off the floor and dress quickly.

I take in John's sleeping face one more time before slipping silently out the door. In the living room, I grab my heels and purse off the floor, ducking out of his apartment.

To the doorman's credit, he doesn't even blink as he opens the door for me. I slink out into the night, barefoot and obviously doing a middle-of-the-night walk of shame.

I recall that John's apartment is very close to mine, and under normal circumstances, I'd just walk the few blocks to my place. But it's Chicago – in the middle of the night – and I really don't want to put those heels back on, so I use my phone to summon an Uber instead.

When I crawl into the back of the car, I notice the time on the dashboard – it's just after 4:00 a.m. I'm full of adrenaline and dying to wake Jen up and tell her everything when I get home, but I know she'd kill me for interrupting her sleep.

Back in my apartment, I immediately pour myself a glass of water and run a bath. I scrape my hair into a bun on top of my head, before sinking into the hot water, letting it wash John's touch, his lips, off my body.

I allow myself one glorious moment to relive last night. John's hands on me, his mouth kissing mine, his tongue, his... I shiver with delight, lowering myself deeper into the steamy water.

But how am I supposed to face him? What was I thinking, sleeping with the owner of my company? He's practically my boss. Even if it is John, the guy from high school I never really got over.

Don't get me wrong, I knew what I was doing. I'd had a few drinks, but it was just enough to make me feel brave and uninhibited. I made a choice, and for the most part I don't regret it.

But the thought of seeing John in the office on Monday makes me so anxious I could throw up. What if he does this with all of his employees? What if he has slept his way through the entire office?

I don't really think that he's like that, based on what I've seen and the kind of man he is. But how would I know?

What if he thinks I only slept with him to advance my career? Or to pay him back, in a sense, for the money he gave me? I would never do anything like that, and the thought of him thinking that way about me makes me ill.

Maybe we went too far, too fast. We should have talked more, established some boundaries, and decided if this was the best idea considering we work together.

Once I'm out of the tub, I pull on my softest sweatpants and an oversized t-shirt. The familiarity of my own bed is comforting, and I'm surprised at how tired I am once my head hits the pillow, despite the nerves buzzing through my body. My last thought before I fall asleep is how nice it was to have John's arms wrapped around me, and how I kind of wish I was still in bed with him, in spite of everything.

———

I wake up to a pounding at my apartment door while my cell phone buzzes from my nightstand.

I jump out of bed to answer the door, knowing there's only one person it could be.

"Somebody didn't sleep at home last night!" Jen crows, pushing past me into my apartment. She looks fresh-faced and ready to take on the day, and she's carrying a large paper sack and a drink carrier. "I brought bagels and coffee!"

"Oh, thank God," I moan, reaching for the bag.

"Not so fast," Jen chides playfully, pulling the bag out of my reach. "Spill first! I came over after work last night to see if you wanted to hang out, but *you weren't here.* I left you a note and went out dancing with some of the girls from work, and when I came home super late, I saw the note was still on your door. So, where the heck were you, if you weren't at home in your own bed after midnight, hmmm?"

"Sustenance and caffeine first," I plead. "Then I'll tell you everything, I swear."

"Fine," Jen sighs, handing over the food. "But this better be good!"

We settle on my couch, where I curl up under a throw blanket and dig into a bagel sandwich.

"Oh, God, that's good," I moan after I take the first bite.

"Okay, now, enough procrastinating! Tell me what you were up to last night, I'm dying over here!"

I try to come up with the best way to say it, but I can't hold back any longer. I need to gossip, and I'm dying for Jen's advice.

"I slept with John," I blurt, without preamble.

"*What?!*"

"I said I—"

"John *McQueen?!*"

"Yeah, he—"

"*Your BOSS John?!*"

"Well, yeah, but—"

"*JOHN MCQUEEN FROM HIGH SCHOOL?!*"

I wait for Jen to digest the news before launching into the story. I explain how he invited me for happy hour with the work crew, and that we were the last ones to leave the bar. I tell her how John apologized for the way he treated me in high school, and we cleared up the sign-on bonus situation. I give her all the details... how he asked me back to his place, ostensibly to reminisce about high school days.

...how we had tender, passionate sex, although I don't tell her every little detail about that.

"Was it good?" Jen asks, wiggling her eyebrows at me over her cup of coffee.

"Better than good," I answer with a shit-eating grin.

"Good for you." Jen nods appreciatively, then goes silent.

"What?"

"Nothing, it's just... so what now?" Jen asks.

"What do you mean?"

"I mean, what happens next? It's not like this is some random one-night stand. Not only is he someone you've known for a long time, which already complicates things, but he's your freaking *boss*. And didn't you tell me he has a kid? Is the baby mama still in the picture, or what's up with that? Are you guys dating now, or—"

"I don't know!" I cry, covering my head with the blanket. "I don't know, I don't know!"

"I'd feel awkward as hell going into work if I slept with my boss," Jen comments, rather unhelpfully.

"I *do* feel awkward," I agree. "So much so that I kind of... snuck out in the middle of the night."

"You *what?*"

"I was nervous!" I rationalize. "I woke up in the night, and everything just sort of hit me at once. I freaked out."

"Do you regret it?" Jen asks, watching my face carefully while I answer.

"Yes and no," I say honestly, taking a contemplative sip of my coffee. "He was a gentleman, and there was definitely a spark between us. Sure, we were drinking, but we weren't *that* drunk. I wanted to sleep with him. But there's no getting around it – he *is* my boss."

I hear my phone buzzing from the bedroom. Jen and I look at each other, and Jen verbalizes exactly what I'm thinking: "What if that's him?"

Before I can stop her, she leaps off the couch and dashes into my bedroom to grab the phone.

"It's a text!" she yells, bringing the phone back to the couch.

"What does it say?" I wince, preparing myself.

Jen smirks as she reads, "Hey, sexy lady – where'd you go? I was hoping we could have coffee together today."

"Oh, God," I say, both guilty and embarrassed. How would I have felt if it had been the other way around, and John had ditched me in the middle of the night after sleeping together?

It's not that I'm not into him – that's exactly the problem. I'm *too* into him, and with John being my boss, that can't be a good thing.

And although I've seen plenty of evidence since working at Room that John is a changed man, I'm still not sure that I can trust him not to hurt me.

I explain all of this to Jen, who nods along in agreement.

"So, what are you going to say back to him?" she questions gently.

"I don't know. What would you do?"

Jen sighs, then takes a moment to think. "I honestly don't know," she admits. "It's a complicated situation. I guess the biggest thing for me would be not jeopardizing my job, especially right after getting laid off. But I know you have feelings for him, and he's more than just your boss."

"No, you're right," I agree sadly. "I think we rushed into things. We should have talked about this more before jumping into bed together."

"Do you want to see him again?"

"It's not like I have a choice – I'll have to see him at work on Monday." My stomach clenches with discomfort at the thought.

"Duh, but I mean, do you want to *see* him again, like... hook up again?"

"I guess it's probably a bad idea," I reply sadly, realizing this feeling is familiar. It's similar to how I felt after John and I kissed in high school, when I realized that no matter how strong my feelings for him were, we just couldn't be together.

"Well, it sounds to me like at the very least, you guys need to talk about what happened and get on the same page with everything."

"Yeah," I agree reluctantly, not looking forward to what promises to be an awkward and painful conversation.

Before I can change my mind, I quickly type out:

Hey, I had a good time last night, but I think we might have made a mistake. Can we talk?

I exhale after sending it, reading my words to Jen, who nods her approval.

Now all I can do is wait for his response.

Jen and I spend the rest of the day together. We go to a yoga class, get lunch at a sandwich shop, and come back to my place to watch a movie with a bottle of wine.

John still hasn't texted me back.

At least I had Jen to distract me on Saturday. But on Sunday, she has a work event downtown. The hours pass excruciatingly slowly as I watch my phone, waiting for John's reply.

Did I upset him? I know it was wrong to leave in the night like that, but I can explain everything if he'd just talk to me. My fingers pull up his number in my phone at least a dozen times, itching to press the call button.

But he must have seen my message. If he wanted to talk, he would have responded by now.

I stay up late Sunday night, waiting for a message from John that will soothe my nerves in time for work on Monday.

But nothing comes.

I sleep fitfully that night, tossing and turning and lying awake, dreading the confrontation to come in the morning.

14
_____

JOHN

I wake up on Saturday morning with a huge smile on my face. Even though we went to bed late and I had more than my share to drink, I feel like I've just had the most refreshing sleep of my life.

I can't wait to lay around in bed with Lucy, just talking and laughing and being together. I want to bring her breakfast in bed – I wonder if I should just make regular coffee, or run out and get her one of those sugary espresso drinks she likes?

All of these thoughts run through my head before I roll over and discover that Lucy is gone.

I sit bolt upright, panicking for a split second, assuming she left.

But she wouldn't do that, would she?

No, that would be very unlike Lucy. We had a great time last night – or at least, I did – and I did my best to make sure she did, too. And I'm not just talking about the sex. I loved every minute of the time I spent with her. I settle back against the pillows. Surely, she's just in the bathroom.

When several minutes pass and she doesn't return, I climb out of bed, slip on some sweats and a t-shirt, and knock softly on the closed bathroom door.

"Lucy?" I call out softly. "Are you in there?"

Silence.

With a pit in my stomach, I push open the unlocked door, realizing as my gut sinks, she's not there.

I rush into the living room, hopeful she'll be sitting on the couch, wrapped in my bathrobe and reading one of the books off my bedroom bookshelf. Perhaps she woke much earlier and didn't want to disturb me. Or maybe she had the same thought I did and is trying to make breakfast in the kitchen.

But it takes just one look in the large open space to see that Lucy is not here.

My hopes sinking, I try to justify her actions. Perhaps she had plans or an appointment this morning. She didn't mention anything last night, but maybe it slipped her mind. I check everywhere for a note or any signs of where she rushed off to, but all I can see is that any trace of her – her purse, her shoes, her clothes – are gone.

It's like she was never here.

For a second I wonder if I've lost my mind, if Lucy was ever here at all. Maybe I got more wasted than I realized at last night's happy hour.

But then I notice the yearbook, lying abandoned on the floor next to the couch. I pick it up, seeing that it fell face down on the page that has Lucy's photo. I look at her smiling face for a moment, feeling sick.

Because this isn't right. Why did she take off like this? Did I say something, do something wrong?

I check my phone. Surely, she must have called, sent me a text message... anything to explain why she left without a word.

But there's nothing.

I'm at a total loss. This has never happened to me before.

I've slept with my fair share of women through high school, college, and the times when Olivia and I were broken up. Most of them were meaningless flings, or women I was dating casually.

Sex with Olivia was much like being with Olivia in general – wild, crazy, and intense. Up until last night, I would have said that Olivia was the best sex of my life.

But sex with Lucy was something entirely different. Even though it was our first time together, it felt familiar and right. Making love to Olivia was like going on an insane adventure but making love to Lucy was like coming home.

I can't believe that I assumed she felt the same way. How can only one person feel that kind of connection with someone else, and not the other?

I'm disappointed, lonely, and more confused than ever.

Maybe there's still some explanation, though.

I type out a text to Lucy. Actually, I type out several, deleting and starting over dozens of times.

Is everything okay?

Hey beautiful, where are you?

I'm sorry if I said, or did, anything last night to...

Hey sexy lady, can we meet for lunch today?

I hope everything is alright...

I delete and start over so many times, each new message sounding more desperate than the last. The last thing I want to do is scare her off, so I try to keep it light, while still letting her know I want to spend more time with her.

Hey, sexy lady - where'd you go? I was hoping we could have coffee together today.

I hit the send button before I can overthink it anymore.

I turn on the TV in the living room and listen to the sports channel while making coffee, trying to distract myself as I wait for Lucy's reply.

Several minutes tick slowly by. I sit on the couch, staring at the TV screen but not really taking in anything I'm seeing. I drink my black coffee out of a World's Best Dad mug – a gift from Bella for Father's Day last year – and glance at my phone, which is sitting on my lap, every few seconds.

Finally, it lights up with a text message.

My heart leaps out of my chest when I see it's from Lucy.

Thank God.

But then my heart plummets as I read her words, each digitized letter a knife to my heart.

Hey, I had a good time last night, but I think we might have made a mistake. Can we talk?

I stare at my phone in shock for a second. I feel like I've been punched in the stomach. The wind is knocked out of me and my innards are twisting.

Before I even know what I'm doing, I whip my arm back and throw my phone with such force across the room that it hits the wall and falls to the floor with a loud clatter.

I bury my head in my hands, frustrated and miserable.

A mistake. She thinks last night was a *mistake.*

I feel terrible. Did I take advantage of her in some way? I tried to make sure she was okay with everything, considering I'm her boss and that we had been drinking. I thought we agreed that it didn't matter, that we were both doing what we wanted.

Or maybe she's saying that it didn't mean anything, that it was a one-night stand for her. But how can that be, after the connection we had? Or at least, the one I thought we shared.

I'm mortified. I'm hurt. This feels painfully familiar, and I realize it's just like how I felt at the end of my senior year of high school, when Lucy turned me down.

The difference is, I know I didn't deserve to be with her then. I'd treated her terribly and she was exactly right not to trust me or reward my bad behavior. But I'm a different person now, and I really thought she could see that.

Maybe I'm not as different as I thought.

Throughout the day, I torture myself by typing and deleting a million more messages to her.

Can you come over so we can talk about this?
I'm sorry if...
Can you call me, please?
It wasn't a mistake to me...
Lucy, please don't...
I want to see you...
I had a good time, too. I thought that we...
I thought...

But none of the words are good enough. None of them express what I really want to say, how I really feel. I thought we were starting something big, that we both felt how special last night was, that we could work through the complications of our history and the fact that we work together.

I can't believe how wrong I was.

I spend most of the weekend in bed feeling sorry for myself. I'm dreading seeing Lucy at work Monday, knowing that she doesn't feel the same way that I feel about her.

She turned me down – again.

I'm not good enough for a woman like Lucy. I never have been, and never will be, no matter how hard I try.

When will I ever learn?

On Monday morning, I ignore my alarm. I'll be late for work, but what does it matter? What's the point of being the boss if you can't enjoy the perks every once in a while?

Not that I feel like I can enjoy much of anything at the moment. I still feel how I felt on Saturday morning when Lucy sent me that message – like she scooped out my insides. I feel hollow, empty, and sick.

I look at myself in the bathroom mirror as I get ready to go into the office, and I'm a wreck. I haven't showered or shaved, I have dark circles under my eyes, and my clothes are wrinkled from not being laid out the night before like I usually do. But again, what does it matter?

On my way to work, I call Greta to let her know I'm running late.

"Hey boss, everything okay?" Greta answers, concerned.

"Yeah, just running a little late today."

"Are you picking up your daughter?"

"No, no, nothing like that. Just overslept, that's all."

"Oh." Greta sounds surprised. I can't blame her. In all our years of working together, I've never been late for anything, unless there was a situation with Bella or Olivia. "Um, okay. Well, I moved your 8:00 a.m. conference call to tomorrow, and I shuffled a few other things around on your schedule for you, so you should be okay."

"Thanks, Greta," I say, and I can hear the hollowness in my own voice.

"You don't sound so good," says Greta. "Are you sick? You should just take the day off if you need to, you know. There's nothing urgent on the calendar..."

"No, it's fine. I'm fine," I say, unconvincing even to my own ears. "I'm just a little under the weather, I guess. I'll be there soon."

I hang up, sighing, not wanting to deal with Greta peppering me with questions all day. I resolve to go straight to my office, lock the door and stay there. No need to see Lucy; she made it perfectly clear that she's not interested in having anything to do with me.

I'm able to slip into my office undetected, where I send Greta an email saying I think I might be contagious and to tell everyone to stay away. I throw myself into my work, the distraction is a relief from the negative loop of thoughts that have plagued me all weekend, since Lucy's rejection.

I'm so consumed by my work that I haven't even given Lucy, or anything else, a thought for most of the morning, so when I hear a gentle knock at my door, it jolts me.

"Hey," says Lucy softly, slipping into the room and closing the door behind her.

"Hello, Lucy," I say evenly, not getting up from my desk.

"I was wondering if we..." she begins, and it's absolute torture to look at her. She looks beautiful, as usual. She's wearing a blue top that brings out her eyes, and her shiny hair is pulled back in a low bun except for a few loose strands that have escaped to frame her face. I long to jump out of my chair, pull her into my arms, tuck her hair behind her ears, and cover her face with kisses.

But I can't do that.

"I don't know if you heard, Lucy, but I'm really not feeling well," I say coldly. Lucy takes a step back, as if my words are literally pushing her away.

"Oh... okay, I'm sorry. I just..." she starts again.

"Look, why don't you just send me an email?" I say, turning back to my work and ending the conversation.

"Sure," she says quietly, and even though I'm not looking at her, I can tell from the tremor in her voice that she's on the verge of tears. I hear the door close with a click, and I know she's gone.

I put my head down on my desk, in pain. I didn't want to be harsh or rude, but really, what is there to say? Lucy said so herself, we made a mistake. And I'm sure as hell not going to let it happen again. I can't keep putting myself through these feelings.

How could I have read everything so wrong?

The rest of the week passes by much the same. I drag myself into work where I hole up in my office. Any time I see Lucy in passing, I look away or quickly find someone else to talk to.

On Friday morning, I'm sitting at my desk when my phone buzzes with a message. It's from Lucy. My first reaction, out of habit, is delight, followed by crushing grief. Intrigued, I open the message.

· · ·

We really need to talk. Will you please meet me at the coffee shop after work?

I look at the message over and over, but there's not much to read into. I can't tell if her tone is angry, excited, nervous, or what.

She probably just wants to make sure I don't tell anybody about what happened between us, I think dully. After all, she was so concerned about favoritism when she started working here, of course she wouldn't want anyone at work to know we slept together.

Not that I would ever tell anyone. Don't get me wrong, if Lucy wanted to be with me, I'd want to shout it from the rooftops. But regardless of how I feel, I wouldn't kiss and tell, especially not at work. I've learned to be more respectful than that.

For a moment, I consider ignoring the message, but I know there's no point. I can't escape Lucy, and if I don't face her today, I'll just have to do it some other time.

Fine. I'll be there just after 5:00.

I read my words several times before sending, wanting to add more, but there's really nothing to say.

As the clock ticks closer to the end of the workday, I brace myself for another round of painful rejection from Lucy.

15

LUCY

Ever since last weekend, work has been unbearable.

Each day I go into the office with a knot in my stomach, both dreading seeing John and yet dying to speak to him.

I'm embarrassed by how I acted, for running off and leaving in the middle of the night like that. I'm also desperate to know what he's thinking. I need to know how he's feeling, but he's completely shut me out.

After ignoring my message on Saturday, John keeps it up at work, mostly hiding in his office all week. Instead of venturing out for his usual breaks, chatting with the staff, or keeping his door open, now he's locked in his private space for most of the day.

Greta mentioned in passing that he's been sick and wanted everyone to stay away, and it might be true. I went into his office on Monday to figure out what was going on between us, and he looked terrible. I mean, John still looked gorgeous, of course, but he also appeared as though he hadn't slept or showered in days.

When I tried to speak to him, he was so cold, and shut me down immediately.

It hurt. It really hurt.

I don't know how he feels about what happened last weekend, but to me, it was something special. I don't go around having sex with just anyone, and the emotional connection I felt with John made the sex a hundred times better. More meaningful.

When I told him it was a mistake, I meant we shouldn't have rushed into things so quickly. He's my boss after all. We should've had more than just *one* drunken conversation about it before jumping into bed.

I need to be sure that whatever happens between us won't affect my job, because my job is... my whole life. Without it, I don't have an income or a place to live. And it's not just the money – I really like working at Room. I love the projects I'm doing, my little cubicle, the opportunities for advancement, and my coworkers. I can't risk losing it all over what could just be a meaningless fling for John.

Because it's not a fling for me. I would never sleep with a boss unless I had feelings for him. I can only imagine it would make everything at work more complicated, and I would hate for anyone to think that I'm trying to sleep my way to the top. That's the furthest thing from the truth.

When he brushed me off in his office, I rushed off, hiding in the bathroom while I cried. How could he be so heartless after what we did? After everything we had shared?

Maybe I upset him by saying it was a mistake? It *was* a mistake; in that we should have talked. We shouldn't have rushed into anything since we work together. But I don't regret our night together – surely he knows that?

Perhaps this is his way of showing me that he's not interested. Maybe I was just something he had to get out of his system. He didn't get to sleep with me in high school, so he wanted to add me to the notches on his belt now. It's probably a pride thing for him.

Yet, I don't really believe that's him – at least, not anymore. But it's hard to believe that he's a changed man when he's now deliberately ignoring me.

All week, I've been trying to talk to him, to catch his eye. There's no way I'm going to "send him an email," as he suggested, and it's too important to discuss over text. I need to talk to him in person, to see his reaction face-to-face.

By Friday, I can't stand it anymore. John's clearly avoiding me, and I won't get an opportunity to talk to him unless I make one. I send him a text, practically begging him to meet me for coffee after work so we can talk.

His response is terse and cold, but at least he agrees to meet with me.

As the workday comes to a close, I become more anxious. I'm not exactly sure what I'm going to say to John, beyond apologizing for my *mistake* comment. I want to explain myself, and I hope he gives me the chance.

But what if he shuts me down again? Or what if I find out that he doesn't care at all... that I'm just another conquest to him?

Everything about working at Room is perfect, except for this new, horrible tension between John and me. I can't go on working here, dreading each new day because of my feelings for my boss. For better or for worse, a conversation has to happen.

At 5:00, everyone starts wrapping up their work for the week. I rush to the bathroom and run some cool water over my wrists to calm my nerves. It's a trick my stepmom Karen taught me in high school when I was nervous to give a presentation in front of my whole class. The nerves I'm feeling now are oddly similar to when it was my turn to explain the Great Depression to a bunch of teenagers in history class.

I check the mirror and smooth down my hair. This time, I don't take any layers off or add any makeup – it wouldn't feel right.

I walk from the office to the coffee shop in a daze, realizing when I get there that I don't exactly want to consume caffeine this late. I consider ordering a coffee for John, but I'm not sure he would want any, either. I settle for ordering a chamomile tea, hoping it'll help soothe my nerves, and wait.

I sit down at the same table John and I shared before, when we came here my first week of work. I can see the door from here, so I'll know when he walks in.

I sit and sip, nervously watching the door for John's arrival.

16

———

JOHN

The end of the workday comes and goes, and I'm still at my desk, searching for any loose ends I can tie up at work before I leave. I don't want to be rude and make Lucy wait, but I'm not exactly in a hurry to hear why our night together was a mistake.

Finally, I'm out of excuses to linger, so I make my way to meet Lucy.

I resolve to be calm and stoic, vowing to not get upset when she tells me why we can't be together. Again. I won't beg. I won't get angry. I will continue to treat her like any other employee at work, although I might have to avoid her for a while until I can handle seeing her without wanting her.

I pause just outside of the coffee shop, taking a deep breath before opening the door. Be calm, be peaceful, be stoic, I repeat to myself like a mantra.

I see Lucy the moment I walk in, and my resolve immediately breaks when I see she has tears in her eyes.

I rush over to the table – vaguely noticing it's the same one we sat at before. "Lucy, what's wrong? Why are you crying?" I move the empty chair from the opposite side of the table to sit next to her. I rub her back, trying to console her.

I can't help it. I've never been able to stand seeing her cry.

"John, I'm so sorry!" she blurts out, her blue eyes rimmed with red from crying. "I shouldn't have run off like that. I don't know what you must think of me for doing that. I just... I really, really like you, John. I have all these feelings for you, and I don't know what to do with them. You're my boss... I don't know how to handle this."

She's looking at me helplessly, and I can see the torment on her face.

I'm... shocked. This isn't what I was expecting today at all.

I assumed Lucy wanted to see me so she could tell me to stay away, not to confess that she has feelings for me.

Then it hits me – Lucy said she has feelings for me.

I look at her, dumbfounded.

"Please say something," she pleads, her tears still falling.

"I'm sorry. I'm just so confused," I answer honestly. "I thought you said it was a mistake?"

"I didn't mean it like that." Her words are quiet, as she looks down at her lap where she's nervously twisting a napkin in her hands. "I mean, I don't regret what we did. Not at all."

Warmth floods through my body at her words, and it feels like I've just received the antidote to a poison that's been killing me.

"Then why did you say it was a mistake?" I ask earnestly, still not fully comprehending.

"I just meant because you're my boss, and I don't want things to be messy at work. I didn't know what that night meant to you, or if it meant anything to you at all. Because it meant a lot to me." She gazes into my eyes, seriousness written on her face. "John, I've liked you since high school, and I don't know how I can continue on at work feeling this way."

My mouth grows slack. I can't believe what I'm hearing. This is everything I wouldn't dare to hope Lucy would say, and now here she is, telling me she's had feelings for me since we were kids.

Just like I've had feelings for her.

Lucy looks at me tearfully, waiting for a reaction.

I'm so overwhelmed I can't find words.

I want to take her in my arms, tell her I feel the same way, and explain how miserable I've been since I thought she was turning me down again. I have so much to say. I have so many questions I can't quite wrap my head around where to begin.

Lucy misreads my silence.

"Oh, I'm such an idiot," she groans, jumping up from the table. "Now I've gone and ruined it. I should've known you didn't feel the same way. I'm so sorry, for everything."

Before I can stop her, she darts out of the coffee shop in tears.

I have to stop her. I have to explain my feelings as well. I leap up from the table to follow her.

But just as I reach the door, a woman walks in.

"John!" Olivia exclaims, grinning like the cat who caught the canary. "I just stopped by your office to see you and you weren't there, so I thought I'd check here. I know you used to love this place."

My brain is exploding. My eyes flick from Olivia, to the door, and back again. If I want to catch Lucy, I need to hurry, but one important thing pushes to the forefront of my mind,

"Where's Bella?" I blurt, noticing that our daughter isn't present.

"She's with my mom. It's fine," Olivia says, frowning. "You look upset, darling. Why don't we go to the bar down the street, the one with the nice happy hour you take all your little workers to? We can have a drink, catch up…"

"Not now, Olivia," I say frantically, trying to move past her, but she intentionally blocks the door.

"But John, you never have time for me," she coos, grasping my arm and leaning toward me. "Don't you think we need to talk? Alone, without Bella around?" As she speaks, she draws closer. She's practically whispering in my ear.

A flash of color draws my attention outside, and I look up, finding Lucy standing there through the glass storefront. She's staring inside. Her face turns stony as she takes in Olivia, the woman who's hanging off of me and practically licking my ear. Then Lucy turns on her heel and runs off.

Shit.

Now I've really blown it.

17

LUCY

How could I have been so stupid?

Despite my resolve to remain calm and collected, I completely lost control while I sat at the coffee shop waiting for John.

I just kept replaying everything in my head, getting so nervous about how he was going to react, about what I was going to say, that I freaked out.

John surprised me with his concern, running over and trying to soothe me when he saw me. But when I told him everything, what I meant by saying we made a mistake, that I didn't regret our night together, he clammed up. I even told the man I still have feelings for him after all this time.

I didn't think it was possible to feel worse than I did at that moment, but it only deteriorated from there.

Mortified by my confession, I ran out of the coffee shop. I barely made it a block away when I turned around, determined to resolve this with John once and for all. If nothing else, I needed to know where we stood so that work wouldn't be so tense, for both of us.

But when I was about to step back into the coffee shop, I saw John.

With a woman.

A stunning woman who looked like a supermodel, no less.

Her hands were all over John, and it looked like she might have been kissing him. They were clearly familiar with each other. More than friends.

Hadn't I just left mere seconds ago? How was he already seeing another woman, one he seemingly knows intimately? Did he have a date lined up for right after our talk? Does he get around so much that he can't be out in public for five minutes without running into a woman he's slept with?

Not only did I embarrass myself, spilling my guts to my boss after I slept with him, but then I was met with his rejection and had to see him with another woman.

I'm done with John McQueen.

The despair and anxiety I've been feeling all week have been replaced with rage. With pain.

This is the last time I will ever let John McQueen make me feel this way.

For a split second, I even contemplate quitting my job. I could just email my resignation, effective immediately. I would never have to see John again.

But, I rationalize, I might not be so lucky to get another good job so quickly this time. It was a big deal for me to get the McGregor job, and no matter what John said, I'm sure the fact that he knew me was at least partially why I got the job at Room. If I quit now, I might not be giving up only my job, but also my income, my apartment, and the life I built in Chicago.

Why should I have to pay such a huge price for the mistake of letting a man mistreat me?

Over the weekend, I resolve that I will not only stay at Room, but I will throw myself into my work so fervently, I won't have time to think about John. It's always been my plan to work my way up within a company. One day, I hope to be in Greta's position, or even John's. Maybe I'll start my own publishing company, who knows? What I do know is that I'm not going to let my poor judgment of John McQueen derail my plans for the future.

John calls and texts me all weekend, beginning as soon as I fled the coffee shop for the second time. I don't answer and delete any texts or voicemails without checking them. I would block his number, but since he's my boss, I can't completely cut off communication the way I'd like to.

On Monday, I head into work with a fresh sense of determination. I'm still smarting over everything that happened with John, but unlike last week, I refuse to be shut out. I refuse to display my embarrassment.

By lunchtime, I've taken on a hefty load of extra work. I've asked my coworkers if there are any tasks I can take off of their hands and taken on every assignment possible.

I remember Greta's mass email last week, regarding a fundraiser for Room that's being held in a few days. I know she was looking for someone to help organize the event, and I'd love to be able to put the project on my resume. I search my inbox for Greta's email, and quickly type out a reply:

Hi Greta,

I'm looking forward to the upcoming fundraiser event, and would love to be involved in the planning process! Please let me know what I can do to help.

Thanks,

Lucy

I send the email, pleased with myself and genuinely excited for the challenge.

Greta must be at her computer right now, because I receive her response immediately:

Hi Lucy,

That is wonderful, thank you for volunteering! You're the only person so far who has offered to help out this year. I'm sure John will be thrilled (and relieved!) that you've stepped up. He is in charge of the planning, so please direct emails about the fundraiser to him. Thank you again, and keep up the great work!

Best,

Greta

I stare at the screen and my mouth drops.

I groan out loud, unable to hold back. *Of course* I managed to sign up for a special one-on-one project with John.

It's so ridiculous it's almost comical, but I really can't appreciate the humor of the situation right now.

I can't email Greta now, saying I've changed my mind. She seems pleased that I'm helping out, and I'd hate to disappoint her. Plus, I really do want to work on this project – I just hate that I'll be working directly with John. Obviously, if I'd known that, I never would have volunteered.

It's fine, I think to myself firmly. In fact, this will be the perfect opportunity for me to prove to myself – and to John – that I'm not going to let any weirdness between us get in the way of my career.

Feeling cavalier, I start to compose a new email to John:

Hi John,

No, that sounds too informal. That's how I start emails to Greta and my other coworkers. Maybe a couple of weeks ago, I would have started an email to John that way. But now, the friendliness doesn't feel natural. I delete the greeting and start over:

Dear John,

. . .

Wait, what is this, a Nicholas Sparks novel? Also, now it's *too* formal. I delete it again, then sit staring at my screen for a moment before typing:

John,

There. It's straight to the point, which is perfect.

Now I have to write the rest of the email, and I can't spend all day on this...

John,

I have volunteered to help plan the upcoming fundraiser and was directed by Greta to refer all emails regarding the event to you. Please advise me on how you would like to divide the work.

Lucy

At first, I close the email with a "Thanks," or a "Best," but I'm not particularly grateful to John at the moment, nor do I feel like wishing him the best. I opened the email with a brief greeting, and I'll close it that way, too.

I read the rest of the words back to myself and decide not to change anything. I think what I've written shows that I'm going to continue to be professional and go above and beyond at my job, but there's no room to interpret the email as friendly, or worse, desperate. It also implies that I want to work on the project separately, if possible.

Thankfully, I haven't seen John yet today, but he must be at his computer because like Greta, he also responds almost immediately:

Hi Lucy,

Thank you for volunteering to help with the fundraiser. Can you please come by my office later today and we can discuss the project further?
Best,
John

After reading the email, I lean back in my chair and roll my eyes so far back into my head I think I might be able to see my brain. Of course he won't spare me from having to face him, even after what happened on Friday.

Because, as I'm sure he knows, it's not like I can reasonably refuse his request. No matter what else John is, he's my boss. I can't very well say, "No, I can't walk the few feet to your office at some point to talk to about a project I volunteered to do," can I?

Fine, I think. If a confrontation is what John wants, then it's what he's going to get.

18
___

JOHN

I tried to contact Lucy all weekend, calling and texting her almost obsessively.

I even considered finding her address from her HR files, and showing up at her doorstep to explain myself. I recalled her reference about her apartment building being close to mine, and it tormented me to know that she's nearby and won't talk to me.

But ultimately, I decided that using work connections. Showing up uninvited would definitely fall under the category of "abuse of power" rather than "romantic gesture," so I just kept trying to get her to answer her phone in vain.

If only Olivia hadn't walked in at that exact moment, I think angrily. If only she hadn't been pawing at me when Lucy came back.

I'm not sure exactly what Lucy saw, or thought she saw, but I imagine from her perspective it didn't look good.

The whole thing is so uncanny it would almost be funny, if it weren't so damn frustrating.

I should have kissed Lucy the second she confessed her feelings for me. I should have said something, *anything*, to show her how I felt about her – how I still feel now. I can't believe I let her slip through my fingers, again.

When Monday comes, I'm hopeful that I'll at least get the opportunity to talk to her in private at work, to explain everything.

I'm shocked when I get an email from Lucy, before I even get a chance to see her. Apparently, she volunteered to help plan the annual fundraiser that's in just a few days. I plan it every year, and Greta always sends out an open invitation for anyone to help, but it usually goes ignored. Which is fine – the fundraiser is meant to be enjoyed by the staff, and I like organizing it.

Did she realize that she'd be working closely with me when she signed up for the task? *Probably not*, I think, rereading her terse email and then pulling up the mass email from Greta about the fundraiser. There's no indication that I'm the one planning it, and since Lucy is still new here, it's unlikely she knew I was involved.

I wonder how she felt whenever Greta told her to contact me directly. I almost smile to myself. Again, it would almost be laughable, but I don't delight in making Lucy uncomfortable.

In her email, Lucy tried to get me to divvy up the work, probably in an attempt to avoid contact with me. But we need to talk.

Instead of responding to my email asking her to see me in person about planning the event, Lucy shows up to my office.

She opens the door without knocking and then closes it behind her. After one look at her, I can tell from her face she isn't happy with me.

But she doesn't appear sad or fearful, as she did last week. No, this time, she's looks angry, determined, with her arms folded across her chest and her jaw set.

"Okay, I'm here," she says impatiently, pulling out the chair opposite me and whipping out a notepad. "Tell me how you'd like to divide up the work."

"Lucy…" I falter. I knew she was upset, but I wasn't prepared for this. For her aggressive attitude.

She looks at me expectantly, pen poised over her notepad. I feel like I did in school when I wasn't paying attention and the teacher called on me, knowing I wouldn't have the answer.

"Lucy," I begin again, "We really need to talk."

"Yeah," she spits with a hint of sarcasm, "That's why I'm here."

"No, I mean… not just about the project. About what happened at the coffee shop."

"There's nothing to discuss," Lucy replies quickly. "And, frankly, it's a little inappropriate for you to force me to come to your office to talk about this."

My mouth drops in surprise. She's right, but I wasn't expecting this reaction from Lucy.

"Anyway," she continues, and for the first time her angry facade slips, and I catch the hurt beneath, "You made it very clear where you stand. I just want to do my job and finish this project, that's all."

"But Lucy," I protest, "You have to let me explain. I was just—"

"I don't *have* to let you do anything," Lucy says coldly, her eyes narrowing at me. I've seen her mad a few times, but never like this. It's kind of terrifying.

"You caught me off guard, I thought you were—"

"I poured my heart out to you and you just sat there. After a week of ignoring me, right after we *slept together*."

"I thought that you—"

"And then," Lucy interrupts, holding her hand up to silence me, "Within minutes, you have another woman all over you?" Her voice is rising as she speaks, and I think I see angry tears glistening in her blue eyes.

"I can explain everything—"

"I don't want to hear it, John. I'm done," She rises to her feet quickly. "*Please* have enough respect for me to stay away from me at work. I just want to do my job, okay? Just send me an email with whatever you want me to do."

"Lucy, wait!" I call, standing up, but she's already closing my office door behind her.

I collapse back into my seat, rubbing my face in my hands.

That didn't go at all how I thought it would.

I expected to tell Lucy that I was speechless, overcome with joy and confusion when she told me how she felt about me. I'd explain that Olivia showed up unexpectedly, and that she's my ex and the mother of my child. Just a woman who hasn't quite let me go yet, although I'm completely over her.

I even hoped that I could ask Lucy to be my date at the fundraiser. It would show her that I'm serious about her and that I want the whole company – the entire world – to know she's mine.

But it looks like that's not going to happen now.

My phone buzzes from my desk. *Olivia.* Great, perfect timing. But I can't ignore her calls, ever – what if it's about Bella?

I reluctantly answer my phone. "Hello, Olivia," I sigh warily.

"Hi, handsome," she coos. I know right away I'm getting the sweet, adoring Olivia instead of the snappy, demanding one. "It's so good to hear your voice."

"Olivia, I don't really have time right now," I say. "What's going on? Is it Bella?"

"Can't a girl just call the father of her child to see how his day is going?" Olivia asks innocently.

"I'm swamped at work, so unless this is an emergency, I really have to go..."

"What are you working on?" Olivia inquires sweetly.

"Same old stuff, nothing that would interest you. The most pressing item is this fundraiser I have to finish planning that's coming up–"

"Oh, I remember the fundraiser!" Olivia says gleefully. "We used to have the *best* time at those! It's that big event you do every year, right?"

"Mmhmm," I murmur cautiously, sensing trouble.

"Bella!" she calls out. "Wouldn't you love to get a fancy dress and go to a party with Daddy?"

"What?" I say, snapping to attention. "I didn't... I'm not..."

"Oh, it's going to be such fun!" says Olivia dreamily. "I'll take Bella out shopping today, and we'll get something adorable for her to wear... and a little something for me, too, obviously."

"Wait a second, why isn't Bella at school again? We've talked about this a million times, Olivia!"

"She had a half day today," Olivia pouts. "That's the school schedule, so don't blame me, *Mr. Crankypants.*"

I sigh. Olivia always seems to gain the upper hand in every situation, every argument. But I'm relieved to hear that at least Bella isn't missing more school.

"So what time will you pick us up for the party?"

"But I didn't—"

"Party! Party! Party!" I hear Bella chanting in the background over the phone.

"Yes, honey, a party!" encourages Olivia. "A fun party with Mommy and Daddy, and you get to dress up like a princess!"

"Olivia," I growl, "I don't think it's appropriate for us to—"

"Well, now you've gotten her all excited about it, and you wouldn't want to take that away from her, would you?" Olivia murmurs into the phone so Bella can't hear. Then, in a louder voice, she says, "Daddy says we can go find you the perfect dress today! It's going to be so, so fun!"

As much as I don't want to let Olivia manipulate me into bringing her to the fundraiser, it would be cruel to tell Bella she can't come now that Olivia has her all riled up about it. And I *do* need a date, after all. The woman I wanted to take is uninterested.

"Fine," I sigh. At least it will make Bella happy. "Go pick out something nice for yourselves, okay?"

"You know we will!" Olivia says triumphantly before hanging up.

I stare at my phone, the screen now dark.

What the hell did I just agree to?

LUCY

"You don't think this is too much?" I ask self-consciously, peering into the full-length mirror on the back of my closet door.

"Trust me, girl, it's *perfect*," Jen gushes, standing behind me and adjusting the strap of my gown. "John McQueen, eat your heart out!"

And I have to admit, I *do* look pretty good, thanks to Jen. I invited her as my date to the fundraiser tonight, and as soon as she heard about it, she used her connections in the fashion world to score us a couple of designer dresses I could never afford.

"How did you get these again?" I ask, plucking at the gossamer silk fabric that skims my body, hugging it in all the right places.

"Oh, we have a ton of clothes lying around the office," Jen says nonchalantly, leaning towards the mirror to apply a thin line of eyeliner to her lids. "Designers send us stuff all the time, hoping we'll mention them in an article or something. And we have leftovers from photoshoots, of course, which is what I think yours is."

"And you're sure no one will mind that we're wearing them?" I ask nervously.

"God, no," Jen laughs. "Everyone at the office borrows stuff all the time. It's, like, one of the biggest perks of the job. How do you think I afford half of the stuff I wear? We just have to make sure not to ruin them, and I'll return them on Monday. It's no big deal."

"Have I told you lately that I love you?" I joke, turning around to admire myself from behind.

The dress Jen helped me select is a deep red, almost a burgundy, and the satin material gleams like a ruby. It's a floor-length gown with a low back and a neckline that emphasizes my delicate clavicle. The dress makes my pale skin look more lustrous, and my hair is twisted up into a complicated up-do that Jen spent an hour on. My makeup, also courtesy of Jen, looks professionally applied, making my blue eyes pop and my lashes mesmerizing.

John McQueen, eat your heart out, indeed.

Jen looks amazing, too, in a long black dress with a high slit and a plunging neckline. Her long legs are endless, and her makeup is smoky and sexy.

I wrap one arm around her waist as we pose like models in the mirror, giggling. It feels like prom night, back when we got ready together and even dressed in similar colors to what we're wearing now.

"We're going to knock 'em dead," Jen says, goofily blowing a kiss to our reflections and making me laugh harder. But I'm feeling more confident than I would have thought possible, especially with everything that has happened with John. I just want to go to this event, have a fabulous evening with Jen and my coworkers, and enjoy this event I helped pull off. And hopefully, John stays the hell away from me so I can do exactly that.

Jen and I summon an Uber, splurging and requesting a luxury car – we are going to a formal event, after all. When our driver arrives outside the apartment building, we clamber into the backseat, careful not to wrinkle our dresses.

I'm fine until we pull up to the venue, where I'm hit with a wave of nerves. I look over at Jen as we get out of the car, and she knows how I'm feeling without me saying a word.

"Don't worry," she whispers, giving my hand a quick squeeze as we walk through the doors. "I'll stick by you the whole time. We'll get drunk on champagne, you'll introduce me to some of your work friends, and we can leave whenever we want."

"Thanks," I say, drawing a deep breath.

As we stroll through the event space, I look around, impressed by how well everything came together. John rents out this venue every year; it's a formal event space typically used for weddings. The atmosphere is cheerful and elegant, and I'm proud of my part in organizing the event. It was my contribution to have twinkling lights, candles and flowers covering the tables, and waiters in uniform passing trays of champagne and hors d'oeuvres.

It was also my idea to reach out to some of the leaders at McGregor Publishing to collaborate, inviting their list of benefactors, authors, and other contacts and making the fundraiser a joint venture. Judging from how packed the space is, the fundraiser should be a success.

I've just grabbed a glass of champagne off of the tray of a passing waiter when I spot John striding in. He's wearing a tuxedo, and of course he looks more handsome than ever. My heart skips a beat when I see him.

Then it sinks when I notice the woman next to him.

I recognize her; it's the same woman from the coffee shop.

I try not to stare, but she's stunning. Olive skin, long, shiny dark hair, and the body of a Victoria's Secret model. She has the highest cheekbones I've ever seen, a dainty little nose, and arched brows over sparkling green eyes.

She's wearing a white gown that emphasizes her curves and her long, long legs. As I watch, I spot a little girl in a matching white dress (albeit a more appropriate version for a child) push her way in between them, clutching John's hand.

It's his daughter, Bella.

The three of them look like such a gorgeous picture-perfect family that it makes my stomach twist.

Jen, who has also grabbed a champagne flute, sees me gawking and glances over in that direction.

"Oh, boy," Jen mutters, taking in the beautiful couple and the little girl. "Don't look at them," she commands, elbowing me. "Just drink your champagne and pretend they're not here."

We both down our champagne in one gulp and immediately grab another.

"Lucy!" I hear a voice call. It's Martha, my coworker at Room. She's standing with Jacob, and they both look amazing in their formal wear.

"Martha! Jake!" I gratefully hurry over to them. "You guys look fantastic! This is my best friend, Jen."

The four of us talk, and I'm happy to see that Jen and my work friends hit it off. We all get a nice champagne buzz and mingle with the rest of the crowd. I chat with authors, coworkers, clients, and benefactors. I even run into several people from McGregor Publishing, including my former supervisor, Brett. It's good to see everyone come together in one place, and the night feels like a smashing success.

I've even managed to forget about John and his stunning date, as I haven't seen them since they arrived.

Until the woman in the white dress comes barreling toward me, just as Jen and I are getting ready to leave.

"Hi, I'm Olivia," she says, extending one tan, manicured hand as if she expects me to kiss it.

"Oh, um, hi." I grab her hand in an awkward shake. "I'm Lucy, and this is Jen."

"I'm John McQueen's girlfriend," Olivia says proudly, the slur in her voice giving away how much she's had to drink. "Well, actually, he's practically my husband. He's the one who put all of this together."

"Actually," says Jen, cutting in. "Lucy here did a lot of the planning for this event, as well."

"Oh?" Olivia asks, looking me over again and arching one eyebrow. "Is that so? So you work for John at Room, then?"

"Yes," I admit quietly, dying to escape this conversation.

"You must have worked together closely to organize this event, then?" Olivia questions, her eyes narrowing.

"Not really," I reply quickly. "Mostly through email. John's always so busy. You know how it is."

"Oh, he's never too busy for *me*," Olivia says in a hard voice, her green eyes glinting dangerously.

Before I can answer, John appears at Olivia's side, looking distressed.

"Olivia, I see you've met Lucy Myers," he says. "Lucy is the newest member of our team and has proven herself to be an invaluable asset to the company. She's largely responsible for how well this night has turned out."

He beams at me, and I can't help but blush, in spite of everything.

"In fact, I was just looking for you, Lucy," he says eagerly. "I wanted to tell you that so far we've raised more money than we have any other year. And it's all because of you. I'm so proud and happy to have you at Room."

Olivia watches this exchange with a sour expression. When she can't stand John lavishing praise on me any longer, she snaps, "Let's go, John. I'm ready for you to take me to bed."

She tries to wrap her arms around him, leaning in for a kiss, but he looks at her distastefully and expertly pushes her away.

"Olivia, I think I should call you a cab," he says in a low voice.

"I'm fine!" Olivia shouts, attracting the attention of several people around us. "In fact, I was just going to get another drink! Actually, Lizzie —" She turns to me. "Go fetch me a glass of champagne, will you?"

My jaw drops at her insolence, and I see Jen's face turn red with fury. Before I can respond, John takes Olivia by the arm. "Olivia, I'm putting you in a cab right now." His words are firm. Serious.

But Olivia is stumbling and causing a scene. Before I can think twice about what I'm doing, Jen and I take Olivia's other arm and help John escort her, half-carrying her, outside. Olivia is protesting loudly, continuing to make a spectacle of herself.

There's a line of cabs waiting, and John helps Olivia into the back of one.

"I already called Bella's grandmother to come pick her up. She'll spend the night at her house. Please, go home and drink some water." I hear John tell her. Then he gives the driver an address (I recognize it's not *his* address) and a wad of cash.

Olivia is still shouting at him from the backseat as the driver takes off.

When the car is out of sight, John turns to me and sighs, "I see you've had the pleasure of meeting my ex-girlfriend."

"*Ex*-girlfriend?" I repeat.

"Yeah," he says warily. "We dated several years ago, and she's Bella's mom. I try to keep a good relationship with her, for Bella's sake, but sometimes she makes it incredibly difficult."

Things are clicking into place now, and I'm realizing I've made a terrible mistake.

"John, I... I had no idea..." I begin weakly.

"I'm, um, just going to head home, I think," Jen interjects awkwardly. "It seems like you two have some things to talk about."

I look at John questioningly.

"I'd love for you to stay so we can talk," he says quietly.

"Do you mind, Jen?" I ask.

"No, not at all! We were just about to leave, anyway," she says with a wink. "Call me later, okay?" She gives my arm a quick squeeze and jumps into another one of the cabs.

John and I are left standing alone, facing each other on the side-walk. It's quiet now, and there's an undeniable tension between us, and I'm not sure what to say, where to begin.

"Would you want to..." John asks hesitantly, "Come back to my place, so we can talk in private?"

"Yeah." I nod, both relieved and anxious.

He opens the back door of another cab for me, taking my hand to help me inside. Then he walks around to the other side and climbs in beside me.

"So, that's your ex, huh?" I ask. "She's... um..."

"A real piece of work, I know," John mumbles, laughing ruefully. "If it weren't for Bella, we would have been out of each other's lives years ago. But I think it's important for our daughter to see us co-parenting together, even though we couldn't work it out."

"She seems to think that you *have* worked it out," I comment. "She introduced herself to me as your girlfriend."

"She *did*?" John sounds exasperated. "Sometimes she gets it in her mind that we are going to get back together, even though I've made it abundantly clear that it's never going to happen."

"Oh." My words are quiet. "I see."

"But Lucy," John says earnestly, turning in his seat to face me. Our knees touch, and he grabs one of my hands in his. "You have to know that, as far as I'm concerned, Olivia and I are done forever. She'll always be in my life, as Bella's mother. But I lost those feelings for her a long time ago, and they're never coming back."

I gaze into his eyes, and I can tell that what he's saying is true.

"The only person I have feelings for," he continues softly, "Is you. I was just so shocked when you told me you felt the same way in the coffee shop that I didn't know how to react. I was so afraid I'd lost you again when you wouldn't return my calls or let me explain."

"Oh, John." I lean forward to kiss him.

Our kiss deepens passionately, as we use our lips to tell each other what our words couldn't convey.

When we arrive at John's apartment building, our mouths are fused together all the way to his apartment. From the car, to the lobby, to the elevator, to his door, I can't keep my hands off of him.

Once we're inside, there's no polite chit-chat and drinking like last time. I impatiently start pulling his tux off as we breathlessly make our way to his couch. The bedroom is much too far.

John slowly, reverently, unzips the back of my dress, letting the silk fall into a puddle on the floor at my feet. I'm not wearing a bra, just a delicate thong underneath.

John sits back against the couch with me standing before him. He looks up at me, naked except for my heels and underwear, in awe.

I start to remove my stilettos, until he grabs me by the waist and pulls me to him, mumbling gruffly, "Leave them on."

Soon, his shirt and jacket are on the ground next to my dress. His pants follow, then his briefs. He uses his teeth to slide my thong off, until we're completely naked, nothing left between us.

John leans back against the cushions, as I straddle him with one leg on either side of him. I lower myself onto his stiff cock and watch his pupils dilate as he enters me.

This first time is quick. Eager. We're unable to control ourselves. I rock back and forth on top of him with abandon, with John's hands gripping my sides. It's not long before we climax together.

When we're both satiated, I lean forward into his chest as he strokes my back wordlessly. After I finally kick off my heels, and John scoops me up in his arms and carries me to his bedroom, just like last time.

Once we're in his large bed, we make love again. This time, we go slowly, savoring each other's bodies.

After the excitement of the fundraiser, the alcohol, the outpouring of emotions, and the lovemaking, we are completely spent. I snuggle into John's arms, and he whispers sweet words to me as I drift off to sleep.

And this time, I think with a smile, *I won't leave.*

20

JOHN

I wake up the morning after the fundraiser in my own bed.

Alone.

On instinct, despair overwhelms me. I can't believe that Lucy snuck out on me *again*.

Just as I'm starting to panic, Lucy emerges from the bathroom. Her hair is mussed, her makeup from the night before is smeared, and she's wearing one of my t-shirts.

She's never looked sexier.

"Oh, my God!" I laugh. "For a second there, I thought you'd run out on me again."

Lucy cringes guiltily as she crawls back under the covers next to me. I pull her close, entangling our arms and legs. We lay there blissfully for a while, in that dreamy place between wake and sleep.

Then, I break the spell.

"How do you like your coffee?" I murmur into her hair with a grin.

"Mmmm, sugar and milk, pretty please." Lucy snuggles deeper under the covers, her eyes screwed shut. I gaze at her for a moment before heading to the kitchen; she looks so cute all nestled in my bed.

Instead of the coffeepot I usually use for myself, I dig around in the cabinets for a French press a client gave me once as a gift. I've never used it, but this seems like the right occasion to break it out.

I hum to myself as I heat up the water and pour it over the ground beans. As the coffee sits, I grab a couple mugs and pour milk and sugar into one. I bring the steaming cups back to the bedroom, placing Lucy's on the nightstand near her head. When the steam wafts toward her nose, her eyelids flip open.

"You're amazing," she says gratefully, sitting up and clutching the mug. Lucy moans as she takes the first sip.

"That good, huh?" I joke, sitting next to her with my own coffee.

"Oh, yeah." She wiggles her eyebrows suggestively. "Almost as good as last night."

"But not quite," I laugh.

"No, not quite."

We drink our coffee in companionable silence. As I glance around my room absent-mindedly, the yearbook on the shelf catches my eye, and I'm reminded of our history once again.

"Did you ever think," I say with a smile, "back in high school, that we would ever end up here today?"

"Not in a million years." Lucy laughs, nearly spitting out her drink. "But I'm sure glad it turned out this way."

"I'd hoped it would."

After we finish our coffee and cuddle a while longer, we finally rouse to cook breakfast together. I pull on a pair of sweatpants, while Lucy's still just wearing my shirt.

"How does French toast, bacon, and orange juice sound?" I ask, pulling ingredients out of the fridge.

"Incredible." Lucy perches on a kitchen chair. "Can I do anything to help?"

"You're helping by sitting there and looking pretty," I say with a wink, and she blushes.

"Well, at least let me set the ambience." She stands, moving toward the speaker I keep on the kitchen counter. She fetches her phone from her little clutch purse on the floor (I think it's called a clutch, anyway – to me, a clutch belongs in a car). After tapping on the screen, she connects her device to the speaker, and cheerful music pours out.

"This is nice," I comment, cracking eggs into a bowl. "What is it?"

"It's Cat Stevens," she replies. "Tea for the Tillerman. Perfect morning music."

"I like it."

Lucy joins me, pulling out plates and silverware to set the table. I notice she even neatly folds the napkins, before slicing up some fresh fruit and setting out butter and syrup.

I love how her generosity and attention to detail seep into everything she does, even in these moments.

"Now, enough helping, I'm supposed to be cooking for you!" I scold her mockingly. "Sit your cute butt down and get ready for the best French toast you've ever tasted."

"How can you be sure?"

"Trust me," I say, flipping the hot toast from the pan onto her plate.

I watch as she makes a show of taking her first bite. "Okay, you're right... that's the best I've ever had," she declares with her mouth full.

"Told you." I grin, digging into my own plate.

After breakfast, we watch TV, snuggled up underneath a blanket on the couch. Around noon, Lucy yawns. "I should probably get back to my place. I'm sure Jen is dying to hear what happened last night."

"You tell her things like that?" I ask, looking down at her and arching one eyebrow questioningly.

"Oh, I tell Jen everything," Lucy teases. "So, you better not do anything you don't want her to hear about."

She sees my horrified expression and then adds, "Don't worry, she doesn't get every single, dirty detail. Your real secrets are safe with me."

We stand up, and I offer Lucy a pair of sweats to wear home with my t-shirt. "You looked hot in your dress last night, but I imagine you don't want to put that on for the drive home," I chuckle.

"No, definitely not," Lucy agrees, tugging the pants on and pulling the drawstring tight enough to fit around her slim waist.

"What are you doing later?" I ask, watching her gather her clothes. "You could come back over. I'll make you dinner... or we could go out..."

"I can't," she grimaces, appearing genuinely remorseful. "I've got plans with Jen tonight."

"Oh, okay," I reply with a casualness I don't feel. I'm trying my best not to worry that she's running from me again.

"What about tomorrow, though?" she offers hopefully, immediately alleviating my fears. "We could get brunch, go for a walk... you could come to my place this time."

"I'd love to, but tomorrow is my day with Bella."

"Oh, yeah?" Lucy smiles. "What are you guys doing?"

I hesitate for a moment, feeling awkward. I would cancel anything in the world for Lucy, *except* for my time with Bella. I've made it a point to always be there for her when I said I would, and I don't want to change that.

"I'd invite you along, but first she has a birthday party for another kid in her group at preschool, which I can't imagine would be much fun for you. Then I promised to take her to see some new animated movie she's been begging to see."

I'm not really sure whether or not it's too soon to introduce Lucy to Bella. I know how committed I am to Lucy, but I'm not sure how she feels. And I haven't ever introduced Bella to another woman, largely because I haven't dated anyone seriously since Olivia and I broke up. I don't want to push Bella and Lucy on each other, for both of their sakes.

"Oh, no, I wouldn't want to take away from your time with Bella," Lucy says quickly. "I guess I'll just have to wait until Monday to see you."

"Okay. Maybe we can go get a drink after work, or something."

"Yeah," Lucy agrees. "I'd like that."

I call Lucy an Uber, and I walk her to the front door of my building. "Thank you for giving me one of the best nights of my life, Lucy."

"What, the fundraiser? No problem, just email me next time you need help with another event," Lucy jokes.

"I'm serious." I smile. "I'm really grateful to you for giving me another chance after all these years, even with everything that's happened between us lately. I... I'm really excited to see where this goes."

"Me, too." Lucy stands on her toes to give me a long kiss goodbye.

I help her into the car, and head back inside alone.

It's only been a few seconds, and I can't wait to see her again at work on Monday.

21

LUCY

The rest of the weekend passes by in a haze. All I can think about is John, and Monday can't come soon enough.

It's nice to not feel conflicted about seeing him… to be able to just look forward to everything at work. Although I think we are on the same page, I'm curious to see if he treats me any differently in front of the others at the office.

I take extra care getting dressed on Monday morning. I put on a silky red blouse, hoping it will remind John of the dress I wore to the fundraiser, followed by the sexy night we shared. I pair it with a black skirt that's a little tight, but still appropriate for work. At the last minute, I wear the same tall heels I wore to the event, since he sure seemed to appreciate those.

I stop at the coffee shop on the way to work, grabbing a macchiato for myself and a plain black coffee for John.

I realize as I walk into work, I have a huge smile on my face, one that John put there after the fundraiser and hasn't slipped since.

My grin vanishes, though, my stomach dropping, when I approach John's office with our coffee and see Olivia, John's ex, standing outside his door.

She seems impatient.

She looks incredible, of course. She's wearing jeans and an olive-green tank top, and her dark hair hangs in a curtain to her waist. On her feet are jeweled sandals, one ankle decorated with a gossamer bracelet. She looks effortlessly chic, like an off-duty model.

I try to change course to avoid her, but she spots me before I can turn away.

"Lizzie," she utters with a smile that doesn't reach her eyes. "How nice to see you again." Though, judging from her tone, it's not nice at all.

"Um... it's, uh, Lucy, actually," I stammer. Olivia is just one of those women who is wildly intimidating, at least to me. It's not just her looks, it's her personality and attitude. She seems strong and reckless, like she might just blurt out anything that comes into her mind, no matter how hurtful.

"Sure," she says, blinking as if to keep herself from rolling her eyes. "Anyway, have you seen John yet? He told me to meet him here first thing... I imagine he has a surprise for me, he's *so* thoughtful like that."

"Um, I haven't, uh..."

"I bet he's planning a weekend getaway for us, or something special like that. We had just the *best* time at the fundraiser, but we need some couple time just to ourselves, especially since we have a child together. Don't you think?"

I don't know what to say. I can't tell if she's outright lying or delusional.

Or, says the tiny voice in the back of my head, John's playing you, just like you thought.

Before I can come up with an answer, Olivia's eyes light on the cardboard cups in my hand.

"Oh, is that for John? How sweet. I'll give it to him so you don't have to wait. I'm sure you have plenty of work to do," Olivia quips, grabbing one of the cups out of my hand.

"Actually, I wanted to—" I begin to protest, but John suddenly appears before us, glancing back and forth between Olivia and me in bewilderment.

"Olivia? What are—"

"John!" Olivia cries, practically leaping into his arms. "Hi, baby! Look, I got you coffee!"

"Uh… thanks," John replies, taking the cup from her, still confused. He takes a sip and pulls a face. "Ugh, what *is* this?"

"That's my macchiato," I interject coolly, grabbing his cup and handing him mine. "This one's yours."

"I was waiting for you and knew you'd want coffee first thing, so I sent little Lizzie here out to fetch some for you," Olivia lies boldly. "But I guess she mixed up the order."

My cheeks turn red with anger. *Who does she think she is?*

"Actually, I—" I begin to explain, but John interrupts with a heavy sigh.

"Okay, Olivia, why don't you come into my office? And Lucy… I want to talk to you as soon as I can get a moment, okay?"

Olivia throws me a smug look over her shoulder as she waltzes into John's office. John pulls a face and mouths, "Sorry," gesturing to Olivia, and follows her inside, closing the door behind them.

I stand outside staring at the closed door for a moment, unsure what to think.

What the hell is going on? Why is Olivia here?

I head to my desk in a daze, unable to make sense of what just happened.

I power on my computer, but find myself unable to concentrate on work. As I sip my macchiato and try to collect my thoughts, my anger grows.

John told me Olivia is his ex, but she seems to be under the impression that they are very much together. I would have thought that after everything we said and did over the weekend, he would have told her off for acting the way she just did. Or, at the very least, shown some sense of prioritizing me over her.

But instead, he put her first, and sent me away.

I'm starting to feel like maybe *I'm* the other woman.

Maybe he really *is* with Olivia. It makes sense; she's the mother of his child, and he *did* bring her as his date last weekend.

As I sit and brood, I become more and more convinced that, as nasty as Olivia is, she's telling the truth.

I can't stay on this roller coaster with John. I can't keep going from the heights of pleasure to the pits of despair over him. He did this to me in high school, and now he's doing it again... and again. I'm stupid enough to let him.

By the time John approaches me at my desk, I'm so enraged that I'm nearly foaming at the mouth.

"Lucy, I was wondering if you could – whoa." John stops mid-sentence when he sees the expression on my face. "Uh, I was hoping you could come to my office so we can talk?"

"Whatever you say," I reply coldly, rising to my feet and following him.

The moment the door closes, I cross my arms in front of my chest and hiss, "I guess you're done with Olivia for today, and now it's my turn, is that it?"

I'm so done with being treated poorly by this man.

There's nothing he can say at this point to change my mind, but I wait for him to speak.

22

JOHN

"Lucy, what are you talking about?" I ask in disbelief. "I told you, Olivia is my *ex*. I had no clue she'd be here this morning, but I have a pretty good idea of what she was up to."

"I don't know, John. She sure seems to have a habit of turning up wherever you are, and you looked like a happy little family to me last weekend," Lucy spits.

"I didn't even want to bring her!" I argue, exasperated. "She boxed me into it by telling Bella we would all go together! I have no problem telling Olivia no, but *not* when it could hurt our daughter."

I let my words sink in for a moment. I can see that Lucy is conflicted; she's wrestling with whether or not to believe me.

Just when things were going so well with Lucy, Olivia had to march in and screw it all up. I've never been this angry with my ex, not even close. Not when I found out she was cheating on me the first time, or the second, or the third. Not when I read her cruel words, how she was only with me for the money. I've gotten past all of that, but this is unforgivable... barging into my place of work, being rude to Lucy, and making her question my character.

I'm so mad I want to smash something. I almost wish I was back on the football field, so I could tackle someone and take out all of this aggression.

But first, I have to convince Lucy that it was all just a misunderstanding.

I can tell I have my work cut out for me, though. Lucy is as pissed as I am, if not more, and honestly I can't blame her. I don't know what I would do if Lucy had a crazy ex-boyfriend who kept showing up, especially where we both work.

"Then why does she keep saying she's your girlfriend?"

"Because she's nuts!" I yell, throwing his hands up in the air in frustration. It's one thing for Olivia to mess with me, but it's another for her to harass Lucy. "She's a spoiled brat who is used to getting what she wants, and always has been. She calls herself my girlfriend, or my wife, or whatever when it suits her, even though I can't make it any clearer to her that we're done, forever."

"Well, why?" Lucy demands. "Why *aren't* you still with her?"

I don't really want to share all the ugly, painful details of my old relationship, but Lucy needs to know the truth. It's the only way she can understand, the only way she can accept that Olivia has to be in my life, whether I like it or not.

"You want to know why we broke up? Why I'll never get back together with the mother of my only child?" All my muscles tense in discomfort.

"I think I deserve to know, don't you?"

I take a deep breath. I've never had to explain this to a woman before; I haven't been serious about anyone since Olivia. Even though it's all in the past, it still hurts.

"We've broken up several times over the years, always for the same reason. She was unfaithful. And every time I gave her another chance, she did it again. She broke my heart, over and over," I say, my voice breaking. "I couldn't even tell you how many guys she was with while we were together. She was never honest. I always had to find out some terrible way. And, according to her own words to these guys, and some things our mutual friends have told me, she was only ever interested in me for my money."

I plop down into my office chair and put my head in my hands, trying to not get overly emotional.

It's not that I still want to be with Olivia; I don't. I'm completely over her. It's hard to be attracted to someone when they've done such awful things to you so many times.

But I was in love with her at one time, and outside of when Lucy turned me down in high school, it was my first real heartbreak.

"Oh," Lucy says quietly, taking all of this information in. I can't tell from her tone what she's thinking.

I look up at her, and I can feel that my face is probably red and blotchy from holding everything in. I've never felt so vulnerable with Lucy, not even in our most intimate moments together.

"I basically bankroll her whole life," I admit. "But what else can I do? She's a good mother, in spite of everything else, and it's best for Bella to have both of her parents in her life. And that comes with a price."

"So, what was she doing here today? She said you invited her, that you wanted to see her."

"I certainly did not!" I say indignantly. "I've asked her a million times not to show up here. She thinks it's her right, as if we were still dating, which hasn't been the case for years."

"Then what did she want?"

"I think," I admit with a sigh, "that she was here to try to scare you."

"What?" Lucy's shocked, rightfully so. "Why would she do that? We've only met once, at the fundraiser! She can't even get my name right. She doesn't know who I am!

"Oh, she knows," I say warily. "I saw her over the weekend, when I went to pick up Bella to take her to see a movie on Sunday. She kept apologizing for getting drunk and embarrassing me at the fundraiser. She was pushing for us to get back together again, and I told her no, and that I was seeing someone else. She wanted to know who, so I told her."

"You told Olivia you were seeing me?" Lucy clarifies.

"Yeah," I say. "I thought we were... starting something. I figured she'd have to know eventually, and that it would help her see that it's really over. I let her come in here to tell her, again, that she's not supposed to show up here without calling first, and even then, only if it has something to do with Bella. I told her not to bother you again, otherwise I'd have security stop her in the lobby from now on."

I watch Lucy's face, waiting for a reaction. "Please, Lucy, say something," I plead desperately.

"I don't know, John," she says, rubbing her face in her hands. "I don't know what to think about all of this."

"Okay, okay, I understand." I try to regain my composure. "Why don't you take the rest of the day off? It's not fair for you to have to deal with this stuff at work."

"No, it's fine, I can..."

"Please, it won't count as one of your sick days. This is my fault. Let me at least give you the time you need."

"Alright," she agrees, heading for the door.

I move out from behind the desk to stand in front of her. Unable to help myself, I wrap my arms around her, but she only stiffens at my touch. "I can't lose you now, Lucy," I whisper into her hair. "Not again. Not over something like this."

"I just need to think," she says pleadingly, still not reciprocating my touch.

"Take all the time you need."

"Goodbye, John," she says, her voice breaking.

She says it with such a finality, I fear this could be the last time I'll see her. What if we can't get over this? What if she never comes back to Room?

What if I never see Lucy Myers ever again?

I loosen my grip on her and lean back to examine her face, trying to memorize it.

"Goodbye, Lucy." I give her a sad smile. "Hopefully not for long."

23

LUCY

As John drops his arms to his sides, I impulsively grab one of his large hands and give it a quick squeeze, trying to reassure him. As upset and confused as I am right now, I still can't stand to see him so miserable.

I leave him still standing in front of his desk, and I manage to keep the tears at bay until I'm outside of the building.

I practically run home, where I rush straight into my bathroom. Shedding my work clothes, I step into the shower, turning the knob until the water is steaming. I find that I do my best thinking – and crying – in the shower.

I let the tears fall and mix with the soapy water, swirling toward the drain.

I feel a lot calmer when I emerge, wrapping myself in a fluffy robe and wrapping my wet hair up in a towel. Then I do what I always do in a crisis: call Jen.

"What's up?" My friend answers on the first ring. She sounds distracted, and I can hear her nails clicking against a keyboard in the background.

"Hey, sorry to bother you at work," I begin.

"Not at work," Jen mumbles lazily. "Working from home today.

But mostly just wasting time on the Internet. I'm playing solitaire now."

"Oh, so you're home?" I ask excitedly. "Me, too!"

"What?" Jen snaps, suddenly sounding much more alert. "But you never work from home! What's going on? Never mind, I'll be there in a second."

Before I can reply, she hangs up. Less than a minute later, I hear her knocking at my door.

"I'm so glad you were home," I say, leading her to the couch and launching into what happened at work this morning with John and Olivia.

She already knows everything else about John and me, of course. I'm desperate for her advice on how to handle all of this. She's not the biggest fan of John, and I trust her to have my best interests in mind. But I need an outsider's opinion, because my feelings cloud my judgment too much when it comes to John.

"Well? What do you think?" I ask anxiously, once everything is out in the open.

Jen sits quietly for a minute. "I don't know. It's a tricky situation, for sure. And as much as I'm biased against John... I kind of think he's telling the truth."

"Really?" I ask, trying not to get my hopes up. I *want* to believe him, I *want* things to work out between us, but I don't know if I can trust him – or myself.

"Yeah," says Jen, somewhat reluctantly. "I mean, you know I'm obviously not crazy about the guy, based on all the crap from high school. But he definitely seemed different when I saw him again at the fundraiser. And the way he was talking to you... and about you... and looking at you... Luce, he's totally obsessed with you."

"Do you really think so?" I ask shyly.

"Yeah, I really do. And that Olivia chick, sure, she's hot, but like, there was *zero* chemistry between them. It seemed like he couldn't stand to be around her. I still don't really understand why he brought her as his date."

I explain what John said about Olivia manipulating him into

bringing her, and how he only agreed because he didn't want to disappoint Bella.

"I can see that," Jen replies, nodding. "I mean, she seemed pretty nuts, right? And since they have a kid together and everything, it makes sense that he kind of has to put up with her, you know?"

"Yeah, I guess you're right."

"You really like him, don't you?"

"Yes," I whisper. "I really do."

"Do you… love him?"

"I think so," I confess in a rush. "I know it's crazy. It's way too soon, but I feel like I've known him forever. And in a way, I kind of have. It's like the years since high school didn't count, and we're starting over, but he's so different now – he's changed, for the better."

"Well, then, why are you overthinking everything?" Jen demands. "Text him right now and meet up to talk things over. You can work this out."

"I hope so," I murmur, pulling out my phone.

"You deserve this," Jen adds firmly. "You deserve to be with someone who makes you feel excited, who you care about this much. I understand why you're afraid, but I think it's time to let go and let him in."

"You're right. I can't be so scared to trust him, otherwise it will never work."

"Exactly! So what are you waiting for? Send him a message!"

"Should I tell him how I'm feeling?"

"Yes, but not over text… you've got to tell him that in person. Just text him and ask to meet up."

I tap a few words into a new message and read it to Jen before sending:

I really want to see you. Can we get a drink together when you're off work?

"Perfect! Now, go get him, tiger!"

"Well, I can't go get him just yet," I joke, pressing the send button. "He has to finish work, at least. And it might take him a while to respond—"

But before I can finish my sentence, my phone buzzes.

Leaving work now. How about the happy hour place by the office?

"He wants to meet now!" I squeal, jumping up to get dressed. This whole time I've still been in my bathrobe.

"Let me do your hair." Jen heads toward my closet. "It's not like I'm in a hurry to get back to work."

With Jen's help, I'm ready to go in just a few minutes. My wet hair is blow dried and styled in loose waves. I'm wearing a strappy sundress, matching sandals, and just a bit of makeup.

"You'll knock him dead," Jen says with a grin, walking out of my apartment with me, but heading back to her own. "Call me later, and let me know how it goes, okay?"

"You know I will!"

As I rush along the busy sidewalk to meet John, I feel so much lighter, freer. I can't believe what a roller coaster this day has been. I felt so optimistic this morning, only to plummet into the depths of despair. Now, after talking to Jen and taking some time to reflect, I feel confident that John is the man I think he is.

I take a deep breath outside of the bar before pushing the door open. I see John right away, sitting at a small table in the same corner where we spent our office happy hour in. His head is in his hands, and he looks like a wreck.

When he looks up and sees me, though, his expression shifts. A smile lights up his face, washing away any trace of insecurity.

I sit down across from him, returning his grin.

"So," I begin, beaming.

"So..." he encourages.

"I did some thinking."

"And?"

"And I decided that I have to let go of the past."

"What do you mean?" John brows dip.

"I mean," I sigh, "I have to let go of what happened in high school. That was years ago, and neither of us is the same person that we were then."

"Well," John says thoughtfully. "You're more or less the same. You were always mature, even back then. But I'd like to think I'm a lot less of a dick."

"I think so, too," I laugh. "And it's not just that. I have to let go of your past, too. I have to accept that Olivia is part of your past, and that she's going to be around, no matter what. Everyone has exes, and I can't let her keep me from being happy with you."

"Being happy... *with* me?" John repeats, reaching across the table to grab my hands in his. "Does that mean what I think it means?"

"Well, that depends," I tease. "What do you think it means?"

"It means that you're my girlfriend. Officially. And I want everyone to know it; Olivia, Bella, everybody at work, my parents, your parents—"

"Whoa!" I joke, trying to hide how ecstatic his words make me. "One thing at a time! Girlfriend, officially, yes. But maybe... the parents and stuff can wait."

"Sure, sure. No need to rush. I've loved you for twelve years now, no need to speed things up now."

"What did you say?" I ask breathlessly. Surely I misheard him.

"I said," John speaks slowly gazing deep into my soul. "I love you, Lucy."

24

JOHN

When I receive Lucy's message, I leave work immediately to meet her. I'm not getting anything done at work anyway; I'm too distracted by what happened that morning. I'm too anxious about what Lucy is thinking.

Dammit, Olivia. No matter what happens, I resolve from here on out to establish firm boundaries with her. I can't have her driving Lucy away and ruining every chance I have at happiness.

I sit at a table in the bar, waiting nervously for Lucy. I can't tell much from the tone of her message, and I'm not sure whether it's a good sign that she's ready to talk this quickly. I thought she would at least want to sleep on it. But I'm glad she wants to talk now, because I'm not sure how long I can stand the torment of waiting.

This is it, I think, *this will make or break Lucy and me.*

If she doesn't believe me, or if she decides my dynamic with Olivia and Bella is too complicated, then it could be over.

I'm starting to lose hope. I've convinced myself that Lucy only wants to meet to end things in person.

When she walks in the bar, the light behind her illuminates her hair and skin. She glows like an angel. Her yellow sundress flutters around her, and her serene expression completes the image.

I feel the corners of my lips curve upward, though I'm still terrified. I can't help but smile when Lucy's around.

When she sits across from me, Lucy tells me she believes me and that she wants to work things out. She wants to put all the bad behind us.

I... can't believe it. It seems too good to be true.

I'm so shell-shocked I blurt out my feelings for her. Right here in the busy bar.

"I love you, Lucy."

I figure there's no reason to hold back now, not after we've come this far.

Lucy blinks, stunned, and I'm afraid I've blown it.

I know it's too soon. I know it's insane. But I've never felt about anyone – not even Olivia – the way that I feel about Lucy. I don't want any more miscommunication or anything else to come between us. She has to know how I feel.

Finally, she opens her mouth to speak, and I brace myself for her to awkwardly brush me off, to give me some line about how she wants to take thing slow.

"I love you too, John," she whispers, tears forming in her eyes.

"You... you do?"

"Yes," she confirms with a grin. "In fact... I'm pretty sure I've loved you for the last twelve years, too."

I'm speechless. Leaning across the table, I grip her face and devour that beautiful mouth.

We pull apart when other patrons at the bar start to whistle at us.

"Get a room!" someone shouts good-naturedly.

Lucy hears it and laughs.

"Well, should we?" I arch one eyebrow at her questioningly. We're both smiling goofily at each other.

"Should we what?"

"Do what they said, get a room," I joke.

"Hmmm..." Lucy pretend to consider it carefully. "I know a place nearby we can go. The owner has some pretty good top-shelf tequila."

"Oh, right. I think I know that place, too.

Lucy and I rise from our table, sharing a knowing glance.

We leave the bar hand-in-hand, completely sober yet drunk on love.

When we reach my apartment, I ask, "Do you really want some tequila? I can make us some drinks."

"Maybe later," Lucy says with a coy grin. "I can think of something better to do first..."

And with that, she pulls me by the hand into my bedroom.

I slip her sundress off, admiring her flawless pale skin and her beautiful body once again. Her hands rake over me, shedding my work clothes, until we're standing before each other, naked and giddy.

It feels like the first day of summer, when I was a kid and had nothing to do but look forward to months of swimming, playing with my friends, and enjoying popsicles by the air conditioner.

It feels like a new beginning, yet familiar, at the same time.

I kiss her tenderly, my hands exploring her body as she does the same to me. Gently, I push Lucy back onto the bed so she's lying with her legs spread at the foot of the bed, where I kneel before her.

I kiss and lick her sex lovingly, my tongue moving slowly. Though when I hear her moan with pleasure, I increase my pace. I feel her thighs tense and shake. I glance up, watching her breasts heaving with breathless pleasure.

"Oh... oh... John, wait!" she cries out, leaning forward to pull me up onto the bed with her.

I climb above her, kissing a trail from her stomach to her neck.

We shift, as I sit back against the headboard, lifting Lucy until she's straddling my lap with her legs wrapped around my waist.

Then I slowly lower her onto me, wanting her to feel every inch as I take her. As I make her mine.

"Oh... my... God," she breathes, staring into my eyes.

We rock back and forth, locked in an embrace. When Lucy's close to climaxing, she presses her palms against the headboard behind me and starts to buck against me wildly.

"Yes... John, yes... you feel so good... *Yes*," she screams as her orgasm rips through her. The sight of her losing control sends me crashing over the edge, shuddering.

Sated, I slide down next to her. I face Lucy and let our arms and legs tangle together.

"I love you, Lucy," I say hoarsely, still catching my breath.

"I love you too, John."

We spend a few moments in a happy silence, recovering. I'm so happy right now. I never want to lose this feeling, and I want Lucy to know how special she is to me.

"Let's go away together," I say suddenly. "Do you like the mountains? Hiking? Or do you prefer the beach?"

"What are you talking about?" Lucy giggles, trailing her hand up and down my back. "Go away? We have to work."

"But I'm the boss!" I argue playfully. "And I say we deserve a vacation!"

"What? Now?" Lucy realizes I'm serious.

"Sure! We can take the rest of the week off, go to the airport tonight or in the morning. We could be drinking margaritas on the beach this time tomorrow."

"You're crazy!" Lucy laughs. "Don't you think everyone at work will notice if we both take off work without warning, at the same time?"

"Let them notice!" I wave one hand to brush them all away. "They're going to find out anyway. You're my girlfriend, after all."

"I like the way that sounds." Lucy snuggles deeper into my chest. "And you're... my boyfriend."

"I like it, too."

"Who would've thought," Lucy laughs, "that it would take us twelve years to finally start dating?"

"I don't know about you, but I sure think it was worth the wait," I say blissfully. "So, what do you say? You pick the place. Name it, we can go anywhere. I just want you all to myself."

"We're not missing work!" Lucy scolds playfully. "But why don't we go away together this weekend? Maybe take a little road trip, get a nice hotel somewhere?"

"Whatever you want," I agree.

"Keep saying that, and we might be able to make this thing last," Lucy teases.

"I hope so."

"John, where are we going?" I giggle, fiddling with the blindfold he tied earlier to cover my eyes.

"I told you, it's a surprise!" I can hear the excitement in his voice. "Not too much longer, now, I promise."

It's been about six months since John and I officially began dating, six months since we admitted our feelings. We've barely spent a night apart since, and although it's been a tricky at times, I've never been happier.

Our first challenge was figuring out how to tell everyone at work that we were dating.

"Oh, big surprise!" Greta said sarcastically when she walked in on John and me making out in his office.

"You knew?" John asked as I leapt off of him, wiping my mouth.

"Of course I knew!" Greta scoffed, tossing some papers down on John's desk. "The whole office knows!"

"Are you serious?" I squealed in surprise. "I thought we were being so discreet!"

"Hardly!" Greta laughed. "The way you two make goo goo eyes at each other? Disappearing to take your lunch break together every day? I can hardly see you two, the air around you is so thick with hormones."

"Oh, no!" I was genuinely horrified. "I'm so sorry! I didn't want to make anyone uncomfortable..."

"I'm just giving you a hard time," Greta added with a wink. "I think it's wonderful that John has finally found someone as lovely as you, Lucy. Everyone does."

"Thanks, Greta," John said.

"Yeah, thank you," I uttered, blushing.

"After all," Greta spoke over her shoulder as she walked out, "I'm sure your wedding will be the party of the century, and I better get an invitation!"

John and I glanced at each other, eyes wide with embarrassment.

"Guess the cat's out of the bag, then," John said with a shrug.

"I guess so," I happily crawled back into his lap, planting a kiss on him.

Despite my fears, everybody at work seemed delighted for John and me. There was none of the cattiness or accusations of favoritism. If anything, I felt closer to my Room family than ever.

"Girl, we had you guys pegged as the perfect couple from the first day you started here!" Jacob crowed when I finally confessed to him and Martha. We were at brunch together, and after a few mimosas, I couldn't keep it to myself any longer. Especially since Greta had already made it clear that everyone already knew, anyway.

"You did?" I exclaimed gleefully.

"You guys are totally perfect for each other!" Martha gushed. "It was so obvious!"

"Okay, but did you guys know..." I said in a low voice, leaning in conspiratorially over my plate of French toast (which, admittedly, wasn't as delicious as John's), "That John and I actually went to high school together, and that we had our first kiss twelve years ago?"

"Oh, my God, it's like a movie!" Jacob cackled. "Tell us more, tell us everything! What was boss man John like back in high school? I bet he was dreamy, even then."

"He was," I admitted, grateful I could share these stories with my work friends.

The next big obstacle we had to face was Olivia. She already knew that John was interested in me, but she didn't take it well when he told her that we were officially dating.

For a while, she made things difficult. She refused to acknowledge me whenever I was with John to pick up or drop off Bella, and I know she called and left him drunk messages in the middle of the night. Several times. At one point, she even threatened to contact a lawyer to get full custody of Bella, claiming that she didn't want her daughter around a "stranger."

She backed off a little, though, when she started dating some guy, about a month after John and I got together.

Her boyfriend is a professional athlete, a basketball player. He's away a lot for games, which suits Olivia just fine. She loves being able to brag about her superstar boyfriend, and although I suspect she hasn't really changed her ways since she dated John, I'm glad that she's happy. John and I have both met Olivia's new man several times, and he seems like a great guy. Hopefully Olivia treats him better than she did John.

The last piece of the puzzle was Bella. I was afraid that it would take her a while to warm up to me, but the first time John introduced her to me as his girlfriend, she was thrilled.

"Will you read Madeline to me every day?" she asked with wide eyes.

"Sure, if you want," I agreed. "And other books, too. Like Goodnight Moon, and The Cat in the Hat…"

"The Cat! In the Hat!" Bella sang, dancing around joyfully. "Lucy's going to read to me every day, Daddy!"

"That's wonderful, baby," John said with a smile, giving my hand a squeeze.

I've met John's family and friends, and he's met mine. They all think it's funny that we went to high school together and found each other again now, all these years later. Everyone approves, even Jen, who has gotten over teenage John's jerk-ish behavior.

Now, we've decided to move in together. It's silly for me to keep my place when we spend most of our nights together at John's. We spend some time at my place, too, but John's place is bigger and closer to the office.

It's bittersweet, since Jen and I will no longer be in the same building. It was almost like we were roommates and could see each other all the time. Now, instead of a five-second walk through the building, I'm a ten-minute walk away from her. Which really isn't far at all.

Today is Saturday, and John and I have spent the day together much like we do most weekends: sleep in, get hot and sweaty, and eventually cook breakfast together. He had to go into the office for a bit to work on a project, but told me to be prepared later for a surprise.

I've discovered that John is very romantic, so a surprise isn't all that unusual. He surprises me with gifts, letters, books, and trips all the time. I hate to admit it, but as awful as Olivia was, she sure trained John how to spoil a woman. I bet we are going on a date to some cool new restaurant.

I slipped on a red floral sundress that I know John loves, and little ruby studs in my ears that were a gift from him.

I was just admiring myself in John's full-length mirror (which I guess is *our* full-length mirror now) when he walked in the door with a piece of fabric in his hand and a secretive smile on his face.

"Are you ready for your surprise?" he asked seductively in my ear, wrapping the blindfold around my head.

"What's this?" I asked with a nervous giggle. "Are you into bondage now?"

"Maybe later," John quipped. "But that's not the surprise."

"Then what is it?" I asked as he led me from the apartment to the parking garage.

"If I told you, then it wouldn't be a surprise, now, would it?"

Now, I'm sitting anxiously in the passenger's seat as John drives us. He has put on a playlist of all of our favorite songs, and we're both singing along to them loudly, and badly.

"But seriously, John, where are we going?" I ask after we've been in the car for much too long to just be going to a restaurant in the city.

"Is the blindfold bothering you?" John asks anxiously. "You can take it off if you want, but then you'll ruin the surprise…"

"No, no, I've come this far," I laugh. "I'm just getting curious, that's all."

"Not much longer now, I swear," John promises. "About ten more minutes, maybe."

Finally, I feel the car roll to a stop. John parks and hops out of the car. I assume he's running over to my side. Then right's right there, opening my door and helping me out of my seat.

I can hear crickets chirping, and I smell freshly cut grass. I have absolutely no idea where we are.

We walk for a bit, John holding my arm and guiding me. I'm about to die of curiosity when he finally says, in a voice that sounds nervous, but eager, "Okay, you can take off the blindfold now."

I tug off the strip of fabric, glance around us, and gasp.

We're standing in the middle of the football field at our old high school. It's Saturday night and there's no game, so it's completely empty. The sun is setting in the distance, casting a rosy glow across the pristine field.

"Do you remember?" John murmurs, standing before me as I clap my hand over my mouth in surprise.

"This is where we first met," I whisper, tears stinging my eyes.

"Lucy Myers," John says, dropping to one knee.

"Oh, my God."

"Lucy Myers," John begins again, "You have inspired me, you have challenged me, and you have made me into the person I am today. You make me happier than anything in this world, I can only hope to spend the rest of my life trying to give as much to you as you have given me. Will you do me the honor of becoming my wife?"

I look down at him, tears falling from my eyes, my hand still covering my mouth. He pulls a small box out of his pocket and flips it open, revealing the largest and most sparkly diamond I've ever seen.

I can't believe this is happening.

I'm in such shock I can't speak as I gaze down into John's expectant, nervous face. He's still waiting.

"Yes!" I manage to choke out through my tight throat. "Yes, John McQueen, I will marry you!"

John beams and rises to his feet, grabbing me and twirling me around, both of us laughing. When he sets me back down on the football field, he takes the ring out of the box and slides it onto my finger.

It's a perfect fit.

John's arms wrap around my waist as he pulls me close, covering my face with kisses.

"I can't wait to spend the rest of my life with you... Lucy McQueen," he grins.

"Lucy *Myers*-McQueen," I correct him, with a kiss on the nose.

"I like the sound of that."

"Me, too."

We stand there in each other's arms, watching the sun set and simply taking in this moment.

When the sky becomes dark, we head back to the car. As we walk, John suddenly bursts into laughter.

"What is it?"

"Just wait until they get a load of this at work!" he grins.

"Oh, God," I say, rolling my eyes. "Greta was right, we're going to have to invite everyone."

"And have an open bar, of course."

"And maybe, some kind of book or literary theme?" I add.

"Bella can be the flower girl," John suggests.

"Oh, yes! And Jen will be my maid of honor, of course..."

We plan our wedding the whole way home.

I never would have thought all of this would come from giving John McQueen a crazy, second chance.

Life has a funny way of working out sometimes, doesn't it?

If you LOVED *A Crazy Second Chance*, make sure to check out *A Crazy Accident*.

ABOUT THE AUTHOR

Julia Evans is a contemporary romance author who loves writing unputdownable kissing books about bad boys and billionaires with rock-hard chiseled abs. Her love stories are fun-filled and unexpected.

When Julia isn't writing, you can find her running, working out in the gym, reading or watching tiny house shows.

You can find her books on Amazon.